The Diary of

Aaliyah Anderson:

Volume II

A Novel by Randall Barnes

Acknowledgements

Wow! We're already on the second book!

Once again, I'd like to thank my Mom, Dad, my brother William, my li'l' cousin Nia, my aunt Dr. Luciana Green and all of my other cousins and family members who prayed for me, bought a copy of the book and helped in spreading the word about it. Shout out to everyone that bought a copy of "The Diary Of Aaliyah Anderson"! Y'all are the best!

I'd once again like to thank the authors that have guided me along my journey like Allison Randall (Honey), Brittney Holmes, Jackie Hardrick and Nakia Laushaul.

Also, shout out to Mamma Mia and Tex James of iHeartMedia in Macon, GA. Thank you for my first official radio interviews on 97.9 WIBB and V101.7. You made my dreams of being on the radio come true.

Shout out to Dc Bookdiva and the DC Bookdiva Publications squad!

Shout out to Jackson Ra and the Urban Intellectuals/Courting Her Family for supporting me and allowing me to be a staff writer with your widely successful websites. Make sure you check out my articles family!

I'd also like to once again send a special thank you to my original dream supporters Morgan Flowers, Tichina Scott, Tahara Warren (Butta) Tavarius Ottman (Turk), Quintavious Little (Q), Tierra Smith, Saxton Keitt, Shunquez Clay (Shun), Claude Martinez, Tamia Webb, Ta'Quintress Bonner and Michael Hatcher. Also, I want to shout out my class of 2015. We made it! We're finally adults in a world that doesn't care if we live or breathe, something that we actually looked forward to ever since we walked through the doors of our respective high schools. Make your lives meaningful and achieve maximum wealth. The classes of 2016 and 2017 are up next! All the 90's babies are almost grown. Li'l' brothers and sisters, learn from the mistakes we made and be inspired by our triumphs. It's time for us to take over!

I know I'm ready to start my journey at Fort Valley State University the Fall of 2015. I always wanted to go to an HBCU and I finally get the chance! Not only will I grow personally but also in my literary career. Just watch. I'm planning for the Randall Barnes brand to take over Wildcat Nation! Thank you to my fans on Wattpad who still continue to support the Randall Barnes brand. "The Diary Of Aaliyah Anderson" recently broke the 53,000 reads mark and is on pace for 60,000 reads. I'm incredibly grateful for you support!

Also, thank you to the libraries around America that have and will pick up my novels to be in their catalogs. There's still a need for libraries in our community and I, as an author, pledge to forever support them.

A special shout Mr. Farley, Mrs. McRae, Mr. Robinson, Mrs. Brantly-Renfus, Mrs. Green, Mrs. Price, Mrs. Howard, Mrs. Burnette, Mrs. Bruce, Mr. Mccray, Ms. Hunter and all the other teachers, administrators and faculty members that I've encountered that affected my life in a positive way. Shout out to all the folks that I attempted to help and aid in improving their lives that eventually fell off of the proverbial ladder. You showed me that my approach, philosophies and ideologies weren't wrong and directly inspired this edition of Aaliyah Anderson's story. Maturity means learning from the various situations that you happen to get yourself in, so I thank you guys for being my creative muse! ☺

Enjoy the story family!

-*Randall Barnes*

Letter to the Reader

"I guess I got all these folks fooled with how I present myself to the world."
-*Aaliyah Anderson, "The Diary Of Aaliyah Anderson: Volume II"*

So we're back at it again! My second novel and the world's latest look into the life of Aaliyah Anderson. Before anything, I'd like to thank everyone that's been supporting the Randall Barnes and *The Diary Of Aaliyah Anderson* brand. The love, sales, provocative discussions surrounding the novel and prayers are well needed and all of your positivity is what keeps me pushing on.

As I embark on my journey to be a successful, world-renowned author and entrepreneur, I realize how much my writings reflect life and the world around me. I've even seen some of the things I write about in my novels and articles come true! I realize that I have a gift and I promise to always keep it real and reflect what's really going on in the world through the eyes of characters who appear larger than life but still are relatable and realistic because of their respective flaws and experienced setbacks.

From what I see, Aaliyah is now a heralded figure. Her personality and ideologies have outgrown the confines of the book. Aaliyah's take charge attitude and unshakable ambition is almost infectious. She's inspired thousands of people around the nation, and even the world, to achieve prosperity in their lives without fear of the hatred, doubt and scorn of the individuals around them. As Aaliyah Anderson has turned into an iconic figure and brand in her own right in the real world, she's also touched the lives of many of the residents in her hometown of Willowsfield. Aaliyah is a sure fire winner! But she feels as if she's trapped in her success.

Because of her self-accumulated status and the attention that comes with being Natasha Anderson's daughter and D's younger sister, she feels as if an undying spotlight is on her. Every misstep that she makes is public knowledge and her mature swagger creates enemies out of petty, spiteful females like Latasha Smith. Her own friends are teetering on the edge of insanity. Jakiyah's aggressive, "fight first, think later" mindset is getting her in enough trouble than she can deal with and Allison is really going through it as well.

Aaliyah desperately wants to help everybody achieve their full potential but what do you do when your knowledge is virtually ignored, no matter how right or real it may be? Folks are going to do what they want to do, no matter how insane or stupid their actions may be. 'Kiyah is hardheaded and naïve and it seems like her mistakes will teach her more of a lesson than solid advice. Allison has put on a mask that hides her true emotions and feelings from the world but her problems become apparent to Aaliyah as the story rolls on. How would you feel walking around free and happy knowing the people you care for are trapped in cages hurt and miserable but you don't have the power to help them?

Of course, I go through the same struggles as Aaliyah. As many of the people close to me that read the first installment of the series have said, we're "one in the same". In my journey, I've found that the only person that you can truly steer in the right direction is yourself. You can't force a person to change their mindset. They have to want better for themselves as strongly as you want it for them.

The best strategy is to lead by example. Get your life in order and reap the dividends, rewards and riches of success. Folks will see you, especially the ones that are closest to you. Folks are naturally drawn to winners. When they see you shining, it'll occur to

them that maybe the way you conduct yourself does hold benefits. Hopefully it won't be too late before they realize this fact.

Even in this current society where we crave for attention and in-
stant gratification, carrying yourself with maturity and intelli-
gence like an Aaliyah Anderson still works. You may not
immediately reap the benefits of it but consider yourself as a proverbial butterfly. Your journey may be long but, if you conduct
yourself correctly, your future will be infinitely bright. I'm a perfect example that living by the Aaliyah Anderson philosophy
works!

Thank you for deciding to read *The Diary Of Aaliyah Anderson:
Volume II*. I hope you enjoy and are entertained by Aaliyah's ex-
plosive ending to the first semester of her last year in middle
school. But, above all, I hope to inspire you and challenge you to
think. What can you do to become the best person you can be?
More importantly, what can we do to steer our generation on the
right path?

Signed,
Randall Barnes

♠♠♠♠

Victoria & Lyric

August 25, 2012, 8:24 p.m.

I woke up at 4:15 Friday morning extremely nervous! Even though I said that I'd gotten over my fear of speaking in public by doing the work on the radio with D, it changed when I realized that today was the day of the huge nomination party.

The good thing is that Momma let us stay at her house last night too. After I got up and did my normal morning routine, I went over my notes. Momma and I didn't really write a speech per se, just some notes to help me in ad-libbing on stage. One thing I didn't wanna do is sound mechanical. I told Momma I wanted to put some of my own personality into it and we worked it in.

As I was going over my notes and visualizing how the speech would go, I smelled D cooking some of his signature blueberry pancakes with some grits and meatless sausage. I told D about me trying to be a vegetarian so we went out to get some meatless products from the healthy food market. It smelled great too!

I jogged down the stairs and was instantly surprised. D wasn't alone down in the kitchen. My two fifteen-year-old cousins Victoria and Lyric were with him too. They were sitting at the bar in the kitchen eating grits when I came down. D was still working at the stove with the blueberry pancakes.

I ran up and hugged both of them. "What's up you two? What are you guys doing here?"

"We heard you guys were in the neighborhood and decided to stop by and see you before your big speech tonight," Victoria said to me.

"Yeah, 'Liyah. Are you ready?" Lyric asked me.

"I'm a little nervous, but I'm ready to go." I've looked up to Victoria and Lyric my whole life. They're the perfect example of who I wanna be. Victoria is the beautiful, intelligent cheerleader that won't take b.s. from anybody. She's fearless. Even with her slender yet curvy 5'5" frame, she'll square up with anybody. She doesn't just go around trying to fight everybody though. Vicky likes to keep it friendly.

But if you push her to that point, things will get crazy! Back when we were living in Riverstone Creek and I was fighting literally every day, Vicky would come down and stand up for me. A lot of girls wanted to try and jump on me, but she made it clear that wasn't happening. She was respected around the hood. Even though she didn't live down there, the females in Riverstone Creek knew not to mess with Victoria Smith.

Then there's my gorgeous, classy cousin Lyric. She's the youngest of the Smith family, being ten months younger than Vicky. She's spoiled too! Lyric has mastered the art of getting what she wants, whether it's with major authority figures or in the streets with the different people she encounters.

Everybody loves Lyric! Just like Vicky, she's beautiful. Lyric has high yellow light brown skin. She has her long hair styled in frizzy natural curls like singer Elle Varner. Come to think about it, that's who many people say she favors along with Jill Scott. At five feet, she's the shortest out of all of us, but she makes up for it in her body. That girl is the definition of *thick*!

She has a shapely body with a slim waistline which I heard has the guys around Howard-Jones going crazy, no matter what grade they're in. Combined with that, she has a li'l' swag to her that makes people want to be around her. Lyric has pretty much taught me everything I know about dating, how to persuade people, how to be confident, how to dress, how to deal with haters, and how to have a fly personality (outside of D of course).

It's amazing how they both favor Auntie 'Nessa and Uncle Thomas too. Vicky looks just like Auntie 'Nessa with her pretty natural afro and her smooth, flawless dark chocolate skin. You already know how much I like that! Then, Lyric takes after Uncle Thomas with her light brown skin and green eye color. That and their personalities are the only things that separate them in any way. You can definitely tell that Victoria and Lyric are sisters! Hopefully Faith and I can be like that in the future, after I muster up the courage to tell her the truth.

Honestly, Victoria and Lyric are like my big sisters. If it wasn't for them, I don't think I'd be the young woman that I am today. It was great seeing them before the day started. I needed to see them in order to shake the fear I had in me.

"'Liyah, what have I told you about being confident? If you act like the best, people are going to treat you like the best. The same goes with this speech. If you know your stuff and carry yourself with a confident swagger, people are gonna support you and vote for you because they see you're serious," Lyric told me before eating a forkful of D's fantastic-tasting grits.

Victoria followed up, "Plus, we know Latasha isn't serious. I heard she was at Clarks & Wade's skating rink last night. That doesn't sound like anything you should do before something as big as this nomination party tonight."

"She went to the skating rink last night?" I asked in shock. "It really does seem like she's being laid back about this whole thing."

"And you can use that to your advantage," Lyric told me. "It's obvious that Latasha still believes that this is a big popularity contest. She's not taking this seriously because she thinks that just because she's a cheerleader, people will automatically vote for her. Trust me, 'Liyah, it doesn't work like that. Show the crowd you mean business and they'll instantly respect you."

"So you guys think I have a shot?" Victoria grinned.

"Of course we do! You've been preparing for this all week. As long as you listen to Lyric's advice and give the same drive and determination to this election that you do to tennis and your art, you'll win for sure."

"That advice is good and everything, but I got a surefire way for you to get votes," D said as he worked on the pancakes.

"What, Chef Boyardee?" I teasingly said.

He turned around while pointing his spatula in my direction and grinned. "You know that's not funny, right?"

"Seriously, what's your suggestion? I wanna hear it."

"You should come on my show one morning at Howard-Jones. I heard they listen to us at Clarkson during breakfast and home-room. *The Damon Anderson Morning Show* is the highest-rated show on the station. You can reach a lot of people and gain a lot of support if you come through for an interview."

I smiled. "Thanks for the offer, D, but I wanna do this one with-out your help. Latasha's already trying to call me out saying that you're gonna win the election for me. I don't need to prove her right."

Victoria was shocked. "So you're not gonna use your most important asset in this election because of Latasha? Come on, Aaliyah! That's crazy!"

Lyric defended my decision. "Actually, it's not. I feel where 'Liyah's coming from. Latasha's already thrown out that li'l lame excuse just in case things don't go right tonight. Let 'Liyah get the votes without the extra help for right now. If she needs to go on the show, we can set that up. But, for now, let her go solo."

D shrugged his shoulders. "Either way, it's cool by me. I agree with Lyric, let's see what she can do on her own. If Latasha's coming at you like that, you might as well prove her wrong."

I felt sort of wrong for rejecting D's help in this election, but I had to. Now, that's not to say that down the line I won't stop by D's show, but for right now, I wanna see what I can do on my own. D's radio show is gonna be my last resort. It's my secret weapon that I'm keeping near me just in case something pops off.

♠♠♠♠

The Shocking Moment of the Day

Honestly, nothing during school yesterday was really memorable. It was just a normal day. Dasia actually went on D's show yesterday morning to promote the nomination party and our campaign. She did really well too! I didn't have a problem with Dasia going on D's show. The interview was great and she really made it seem as if we were the best candidates in the election.

Back at Clarkson, I got more hostility from Mrs. Jenkins and Mrs. Rockwell in first and second period. I didn't even give them the satisfaction of responding. They were obviously trying to get me to snap so I'd get in trouble and not be able to speak at the party. I have way too much to lose to let my temper get the best of me this time!

Then, everybody was coming up asking if I was ready for tonight. I swear they were making it worse for me! I was trying my absolute best not to think about the nomination party, but every five seconds, people would come up reminding me of it. I was already nervous. I didn't wanna think about the nomination party until the nomination party. Is that too much to ask?

I got my shock of the day when I was walking to car riders and I happened to pass by the lunchroom. Roxanne and D were in there with workers from Carswell setting up the live DJ'ing system. I knew Roxanne said she wanted to be there, but I definitely didn't know that the whole station and all the personalities were coming too!

I ran into the lunchroom immediately after I saw them.

"What's up, 'Liyah?" she said with a warm grin in her normal energetic tone.

"I didn't know the rest of Carswell would be here tonight."

"See, you would've known if you came to the staff meeting on Monday. Tonight at the nomination party is when we officially debut the concept of Hoodtalk 98.1."

My jaw dropped. At first I was nervous, but after Roxanne told me that the whole station would be in attendance tonight, I was terrified. What if I made a major mistake? Not only will it be in front of the students of Clarkson and Howard-Jones but also in front of the people that I work with!

"What made you wanna debut it tonight of all nights?"

"D suggested it. He said it would be great free publicity for the new station."

After my conversation with Roxanne, I went over to D, who was off to the side talking to this sixteen-year-old rapper that lives on the westside nicknamed MoMoney. I'd heard about him around Willowsfield over the past year. I've even listened to some of his songs. He actually has talent too, but he stays dissing people.

Even though he's a Killa, and the Killas are the deepest set in Willowsfield by far, that doesn't mean you can go around disrespecting everybody. Things are real out here in the streets! We definitely don't need a 2pac-Biggie situation down here in Willowsfield right now.

After I walked over there, D introduced me to him.

"Hey, Aaliyah, I'm glad you decided to come over. You two are gonna be co-workers. Mo', this is my beautiful, talented sister Aaliyah. Aaliyah, this is one of the hottest rappers in the hood right now and a new personality on Hoodtalk 98.1, MoMoney."

He extended his hand to shake mine. "Yeah, I heard about you! You're like one of the best artists in the city. You made the logo for D's show and this new station."

"Yeah, but I wouldn't say I'm the best," I said with a wide smile.

"Well, you should! Those designs are fly! You think you could hook me up with a logo for my show and maybe some artwork for my next mixtape? You already know we gotta do it big."

I grinned. "If you give me the right price, I'll see what I can do."

He laughed, "Alright, I got you. Aye D, if you need me I'll be over there trying to see about this DJ equipment. It's was nice meeting you, Aaliyah."

I smiled and nodded. "It was nice meeting you too."

D gave him some dap. "Alright, Mo'."

After he walked away, I asked D, "Don't you think his image is too much for the station? I mean, he stays dissing people."

"Exactly! That's why I recruited him. This is HoodTalk 98.1! Mo says whatever he wants to say whenever he wants to say it. That's good for ratings. Roxanne and I went over what we can and can't do, so I believe he has an understanding of why he needs to tone it down to be on the air."

"I was just checking. Speaking of HoodTalk, why didn't you tell me that we were gonna officially start it tonight?"

"Because I didn't want you to start tripping. I knew you'd be too focused on whose going to be here instead of the speech, which you started preparing for late to begin with."

"D, I swear. I don't think I'm cut out for this. Momma said she's gonna be here, Roxanne's here, Faith could come down tonight. I don't wanna embarrass myself."

D put his hands on my shoulder and said, "Aaliyah, don't worry about that. You're going to do great! Acting like this is gonna make you mess up. You'll do great. Public speaking skills run in the family. Just look at Moms and me. Don't worry about what the crowd will think. Remember what Lyric told you and you're good."

"Thanks, D."

He hugged me. "Don't mention it, li'l sis. Just know you got this. You got your notes on you, right?"

I pulled them out of my pocket and showed him.

"Okay, you're set then."

♣♣♣♣

Being Honest With Myself

At about 6:30, everything started. When Miss Carter said it was a nomination *party*, she wasn't lying! The lunchroom was made into a dance area with a few of the new HoodTalk 98.1 personalities keeping everything moving. I found out a few minutes after I talked to D that the actual nomination speech would be held in the gym. I went down there and they had it set up really nice. One thing that shocked me is that we wouldn't have a podium to prop up on. My heart started beating really fast. The fact that I had to move around and look confident brought that fear back. At least with the podium I could lean on it and feel comfortable. I decided to go to the library and go over my notes for the speech.

I was in there for a long time! When Dasia came to find me, it was like 8:35. The candidates were supposed to start doing their speeches at ten o'clock on the dot. I knew didn't have spare time to waste because anything ran by Miss Carter and Dr. Wittamore will always be on time.

"Where have you been, 'Liyah?"

"In here working on my speech. What's up?"

"Listen, if I tell you this, you have to promise you won't go crazy."

I nodded. "Okay, I promise. What are you talking about anyway?"

"Latasha was pushing up on Deangelo hard. She was giving him a lap dances and everything. He wasn't pushing her away either."

Even though I was burning on the inside, I just shrugged my shoulders. "Why should I care? He's not my boyfriend. And if he was, I couldn't control him. He can do whatever he wants. Why would you even tell me this, Dasia?"

"Because I didn't want you to see what Latasha was doing yourself and lose your temper."

"Dasia, you definitely don't have to worry about that!"

She smiled and shook her head. "Be real with me, 'Liyah: you like him, don't you?"

I shrugged my shoulders. "He's straight, but obviously nothing different from the rest of the guys out here."

Dasia shook her head. "'Liyah, you're gonna let the past mess up a perfect opportunity for you to get with a guy as ambitious and intelligent as you are by dwelling on the past. What happened with Desmond, Brandon, and Xavier is over."

"Yeah, that's in the past, but I'm not trying to get hurt again, Dasia! I've gotten my heart broken too many times to just hop back into another relationship."

"I know you've had some pretty messed up situations with the guys in your life. I totally understand that. I also understand that 'Kiyah has been harassing you about hooking up with Deangelo. I know it's gotten annoying."

I chuckled and shook my head. "You haven't lied about that one."

"Exactly! 'Kiyah's our girl and everything, but we all know how she doesn't tend to think things through and use good common sense. But I need you to listen to me. I've known you since we were back in Riverstone Creek. We came up together. We're like sisters. I know when you're interested in a guy or not. I see how you look at Deangelo when he's around and I hear about how you talk about him when he's not around. You keep trying to fight your feelings because you don't wanna get hurt again. I totally understand that. But trust me on this one: Deangelo is the one for you. This is coming from your homegirl that's been with you through thick and thin."

I smiled and nodded. "I hear you, Dasia. If it means anything to you, I'm going to the movies with him tomorrow. Just as friends though."

She smiled back at me. "See, that's just proving my point. You've only been talking to him for less than a week and you are already going to the movies? I'm just saying! You two perfect for each other. I can see a definite connection going on."

Dasia gave me a lot to think about going forward. I'm not even gonna lie, I do like Deangelo but I still wanna take it slow. If he's the type of guy we all think he is, I believe he can wait until I'm ready to get into another exclusive relationship.

After Dasia and I finished talking, D came into the library with a very familiar face: fifteen-year-old R&B sensation Alana Weber! When Dasia saw her, she went crazy! Alana is like her number one favorite singer out now. If it was any other time, I would've been acting like an excited fan too. But, of course, things were different.

D smiled at how Dasia was acting. "'Lana, this is Dasia. She's a huge fan of yours."

Alana extended her hand and smiled. "I can tell! It's really nice to meet such a huge supporter of my work. That really means the world to me to see I'm doing something to touch somebody."

D then turned to me. "And this is my beautiful sister, your co-worker for HoodTalk 98.1 and future Clarkson student body president Aaliyah."

Alana and I shook hands. "I've definitely heard a lot about you. You have such a beautiful name! The singer Aaliyah is the reason why I wanted to start performing in the first place, God rest her soul."

"Alana was in the neighborhood and I asked her to give you a few pointers about how to conduct yourself in front of a large crowd. If anybody, Alana could give you some good knowledge."

She smiled wide and blushed after D said that. "Well, I wouldn't say all that, but I can definitely lead you in the right direction. From what D's told me, you're sort of nervous."

I nervously smiled. "'Sort of nervous' is really an understatement. Try terrified!"

"Trust me, Aaliyah, I totally understand. I felt the same way when I did my first show when I was 10. But the main thing is to be confident in your abilities and make sure you keep the crowd engaged. Don't talk *at* them; talk *to* them. That's the most important thing that I've learned from being around all the veterans of the music business, including Miss Carter."

I don't know why, but what Alana said just stuck with me. I don't know if it's because she's a famous performer or not, but it just made me feel a little bit more at ease. After talking with her, I felt a little less scared. I thought to myself, *Maybe I'll do good after all!*

♠♠♠♠

Li'l Extra Encouragement

As I was starting to think positive, I bumped into Faith on the way to the lunchroom. After Alana worked with me, it was 9:35. Now, don't get it twisted. Just because I was hidden away in the library working on my speech this one time doesn't mean I was trying to avoid the party. I'm a true to life party girl! I'm not for that crazy, WordStarHipHop type behavior, but I definitely know how to have a good time.

"Hey, Aaliyah! You didn't tell me you were running for president," Faith said when she saw me.

"It honestly just left my mind with me trying to make up the speech and deal with all the other stuff I have to do."

"I completely understand, Aaliyah. I have to juggle multiple priorities in my life too. I just wanna wish you good luck and let you know you have my vote over anything."

"Is it because I'm giving you free tutoring?" I teasingly said.

She laughed. "Of course not! You're the best candidate in the election. Latasha isn't for real with her campaign and we're all gonna see that in a few minutes. She just wants to win the election for the title. You want to change the school environment for the better. That's why you have my vote."

I smiled. "Thanks for your support, Faith. What you just said really means a lot to me."

She smiled. "Aww, I'm glad I could do that for you!"

♠♠♠♠

The Speech

Just as Faith and Victoria expected, Latasha's speech had nothing to do with her campaign. Honestly, it was her throwing shade at me for five minutes and talking about how she'll host parties and pep rallys so turnt that the "high schoolers will get jealous". I shook my head. That has *nothing to* do with this campaign. Folks clapped for her but it wasn't as many as she expected. And she had the nerve to say she was gonna win easy? Please!

With my speech, I believe I did extremely better than expected. People were even clapping and chanting my name when I was done! I talked about how we need to change the food in the lunchroom (I even talked about the red weave that was in my soup), how the administration needs to put more power into the hands of the students, and how I can lead in making Clarkson a better school overall. But what really got people's attention was my position on office referrals and school discipline.

"Another thing that'll change if you elect me as your student body president is this crazy behavior system. Something is going to have to give!"

People from around the gym started clapping in agreement with me.

"How many people have gotten tired of getting sent to the office for something so random as going to use the bathroom when it's an emergency and then teachers, out of spite, won't let you? Or getting written up for asking an 'unnecessary question'? I mean, what is that anyway? A teacher should go by the philosophy that no question is unnecessary, unwarranted, stupid, or ignorant. We are in school, after all!"

More people began shouting and cheering. I continued on, "But what really trips me out is the fact that you can get up to five days in ISS based on how many lies the teacher tells on the student that they're writing up. You know that something needs to change when you have a student that is sent to the office and banned from your classroom for asking a friend for a pencil to do an assignment. You just *know* something needs to change!"

That immediately got a reaction from the crowd. People were clapping, laughing, and shouting "oooh". Everyone knew exactly what I was referring to! I laughed for a second in spite of the situation that I was in. What once was something that had me so angry was now being used to prove a point.

"The power to deny a student their right to get an education needs to be taken out of the hands of the teachers. That'll be the main goal of my run as Clarkson's student body president. Every student needs to be treated equally no matter who you are, where you live, or where you come from!"

When I was done, the crowd went wild! I got a standing ovation. It really made me feel great that everyone was feeling my ideas. But what made things even better was that it was finally over! ☺

After everything was over and people were filing out to leave, I was giving out hugs, shaking hands, and taking pictures with people. I could tell that Latasha was feeling some type of way about how great I did on my speech. The entire time I was talking to people, she was just mugging me like crazy. I just ignored it though. I didn't have time to worry about her pettiness.

Theresa came up and gave me a huge hug. "Wow, Aaliyah! You did great!"

"Aww, really?"

"Yes! People know that you're not about to play around if you get elected president. If 'Tasha wins, it's over for this school."

"I won't be that harsh on Latasha, but thank you for the compliment!"

She smacked her lips and smiled. "I'm saying though, you and Faith are just too humble sometimes!"

I just smiled and shrugged my shoulders. Maybe that's something else that we personally share as sisters: maturity.

Theresa folded her arms and grinned. "But anyway, you know what tomorrow is, right?"

I nodded. "Don't worry, Theresa. I haven't forgotten about what I promised you. I'm just happy you actually enjoy reading now."

"You and my parents both! It's amazing how one book was able to just turn me out on reading like that. I'm been thinking about our bookstore trip all week."

"That's what's up! And trust me, I'm not going to disappoint you. I'm going to put you up on some books that'll even kill your desire to watch TV."

She laughed. "I don't know about all that, 'Liyah."

I shrugged my shoulders again. "Well, they're still going to satisfy your love for reading. I *can* promise that!"

♠♠♠♠

Telling Theresa

So earlier today around twelve o'clock, Theresa and her mom picked me up and we drove to the Barnes & Noble on the Northside. Momma let D and me stay at her house again last night, after both of our hard work. I did great on the speech and D premiered HoodTalk 98.1 perfectly. It was a perfect treat for both of us. I really believed that we were getting closer to staying with her for good!

When Theresa's mom dropped us off at Barnes & Noble, she went crazy! Theresa went to the Young Adults and African American sections and picked up several books. I had to get her to tone it down because we were on a budget. I wanted to get a couple books too!

In the end, she came out with five books: the two books that followed *Drama High: The Fight*; *Shorty Like Mine* by Ni-Ni Simone; *Hip Hop High School* by Alan Lawrence Sitomer; and *The Coldest Winter Ever* by Sister Souljah. I picked up *Hip Hop High School* too, along with *Love and Lies* and *Sin No More* by Kimberla Lawson Roby. I even got two non-fiction books for a change: *Brainwashed* by Tom Burrell and a book about black people in the media called *I See Black People: The Rise and Fall of African American-Owned Television and Radio* by Kristal Brent.

After we got finished, we walked over to the coffee shop located next door to Barnes & Noble to get some strawberry and banana blended smoothies. I actually found out it was black owned too. That made us going by there and supporting it even better!

Theresa was so appreciative of our trip, which sort of surprised me. It was definitely a change from how cold she was acting back when Allison and I were at her house.

"Thank you so much for buying these books for me Aaliyah. I *promise* I'm going to read all of them! Hopefully I can finish them by the end of the week."

I smiled. "That's great! You know buying the books was only the first part of our li'l' agenda. Now it's time for us to talk!"

She nervously smiled and looked down at her smoothie. "Oh yeah. Ask me whatever you want about me and my life. I'll keep it real."

I smirked. "Ok then. Why were you giving me such a hard time when I was trying to help you with your book report?"

She sipped on her smoothie and then said, "Well…one thing you should know about me is that I'm a natural born hater. I know it's petty and childish but I don't like when I feel like other females are out shining me."

"Ok, what does that have to do with me?"

She smacked her lips and smiled. "Come on now! You're Aaliyah Anderson! Everybody in 7th grade is always talking about you. The guys talk about how good you look and the girls talk about your outfits and how fly you carry yourself. Faith definitely talks about you all the time."

I dropped my mouth in awe. "Really?"

"Yes! That's why I introduced her to you. That girl looks up to you. So, when my parents called you to babysit my brothers and help me on the book report, I really felt some type of way about it. Besides, I thought you were gonna be all conceited and stuck up."

I shook my head and smiled. "You were wrong about that one."

She looked me in the eye and said, "I know and I apologize for treating you like that. You definitely didn't deserve that. I really gotta get my attitude and insecurities under control."

"You just brought up something I wanted to ask you about too. Why are you so insecure and on edge? You seem to have a great life."

She shrugged her shoulders. "I don't even know. I guess it's because I have low self-esteem. I mean, I know I look good and all but I just don't feel like I'm the best. I just don't know."

"Believe me Theresa, there's no reason for you to feel down about yourself. You need to believe you got it going on because you do!"

She smiled. "Thank you for saying that! I see why everybody looks up to you now, Aaliyah. You're so positive. You're who all of the young girls out here want to be when we get ourselves together."

I shook my head. "All of you admire me so much but you don't understand the struggles I have to go through daily."

She looked at me like I was crazy. I guess I got all these folks fooled with how I present myself to the world.

"For real?"

"Yup. Like I told you, my family situation is all messed up. What my Momma told me on Thursday is a perfect example of it. She informed me that I have a half-sister that goes to Clarkson with us."

Her jaw dropped in awe. "Stop lying! Are you serious?"

"I'm dead serious. I know my mom wouldn't play around about that, especially with how my father played her."

"So do you know who your half-sister is?"

I sipped on my smoothie and said. "Yup, I know exactly who she is."

Theresa's eyes lit up. "Really? Maybe I could help you link up with her! Do I know her?"

I chuckled to myself. "You know her very well."

"Are you serious? I know her?"

I nodded. She smiled and said, "Well, who is it?"

"If I tell you, I need to promise you won't tell her. I wanna do it myself."

"Aaliyah, I swear on everything I won't tell. Now who is it?"

I sighed. "It's Faith."

When I said Faith's name, her jaw dropped in shock again. "Are you serious?"

"I wouldn't play like this, Theresa."

She sat back in her chair and said, "Wow! You really just surprised me right there."

I shook my head. "I know."

"Well, when are you gonna tell her?"

I shrugged my shoulders. "That's the problem. I honestly don't know when I'm gonna tell her the news. I know I have to tell her, but to be truthful, I'm afraid to."

"What are you afraid of, Aaliyah?"

I sighed again. "That she won't accept me after finding out who I really am to her. I mean, I know our 'father'. I live in his house and I feel miserable. Seeing that Faith doesn't know 'Coach Anderson' is her dad makes me feel even worse."

Theresa shook her head. "Don't even worry about that. Trust me, Faith is gonna be crazy happy when you tell her the news. Like I said, she looks up to you already. This is perfect for her, especially with how messed up her end of the family situation is. It's not your fault things are like this anyway."

"You really think so?"

"Of course! Faith isn't a person that holds grudges, as you can see. She even said she forgives Coach Anderson for not being in her life, even though she doesn't know all the details yet. You'll be surprised how chill she is. Her snapping and flying off the handle isn't something she'd normally do. You have nothing to worry about."

After she said that, I smiled. Talking to Theresa about things really made me feel better. But I still wasn't quick to tell Faith anything yet. Even though it seemed as if Theresa dismissed the importance of this odd situation, I haven't. When I tell Faith that I'm her big sister, I want it to be special to both of us. It can't just be a hallway run-in confession either.

"Hey Faith, you know you're my half-sister right? Yup, our dad is the lying cheater himself, Howard-Jones head coach Ron Anderson! Anyways, let me go on and get to class before the bell rings!"

Yeah, that's not gonna work out…

The Smith Women's Family Standards

After we were done at the bookstore, our moms came to get us. Theresa went back to the west side, reassuring me that she's going to read every book I bought her by the end of the week. Momma took me to her house so I could regroup until it was time to go and pick up Deangelo so we could go to the movies.

As we drove to Brentwood in Momma's nice-looking all-black 2011 Chevy Suburban, she turned down the radio and asked me, "So when were you gonna tell me that you were going on a date?"

I looked at her, puzzled. "How'd you know that?"

She grinned and said, "I happened to hear you talking about it on the phone last night with Dasia."

 "Well, I'm not technically going on a date! We're just going to see *Sparkle* as friends. It's nothing more, nothing less for the moment."

She smiled and said, "See, 'Lili, I knew it! You said 'for the moment'! You like this guy, don't you?"

I blushed. "Maybe."

"I knew it had to be something because usually Saturdays are reserved for going to the mall, playing tennis, or just resting until Sunday. Movies are never in the plan! That's a Friday activity."

I grinned. "Maybe they were just in the plans today."

She smacked her lips. "I'm not buying that! So, what is it about this guy---"

"His name is Deangelo."

Momma laughed. "Alright, my bad! So what is it about Deangelo that you like so much?"

"Well, he's cute, cool, funny, and smart. Then he's a true gentleman but not gentlemanly to the point that it's scary and he tries my independence. He has swag out of this world too, and I'm not just talking about how he dresses. Honestly, he's different. But I'm not trying to jump into any relationships too quickly. For all I know, this could be a front."

"Oh, Aaliyah, stop being paranoid about dating! You had a few rough relationships in the past. It's time to grow from them and not make those same mistakes again. That's something you can use outside of the dating arena too."

I was surprised that Momma told me that! "I thought I was avoiding my past mistakes by taking things slow."

"No, you're making an even bigger mistake. I understand that you're being cautious of the young men you date, but you're taking it too slow. It usually takes a week for you to know whether you're gonna end up with a guy or not. They know that too. After a week, they'll believe you're not feeling them and move on, especially on the teenage dating scene. There's not many true up and down good guys to choose from. Most of the boys around your age down here in Willowsfield are either thugs or players trying to get a quick fix - or both! It's rare to see a guy like how you described Deangelo."

"So what do you think I should do?"

"First, let me meet him. I wanna make sure you're going out with a guy that truly has his head on his shoulders instead of a Chief Keef-type guy."

I laughed. "Momma are you serious?"

"Of course! I'm gonna make sure he's up to the Smith women's family standards. If he's not, all of what I just said goes out of the window."

"But what if he is?"

"Then I'd approve of you going with him. He has to get approved first."

"Momma, I'm still tripping out about what you said about making sure I'm not dating a Chief Keef-type guy!" I said still laughing.

She smiled. "Come on, Aaliyah! I may be thirty-four, but I definitely wasn't born yesterday. Plus, I work in radio. How would it look if I didn't know about a newer artist, no matter how good or bad he is?"

♠♠♠♠

A Relationship Blossoms

The movie trip was a whole lot of fun! Deangelo really impressed Momma. She was asking him questions like he was doing an interview on one of her shows! But he didn't get overwhelmed and still kept it cool.

When Deangelo got out to pay for our tickets, Momma said before I hopped out of the car, "Aaliyah, he's a keeper. Deangelo is the right one for you. I don't see a lot of fourteen-year-old boys that mature and goal-minded. I believe you really should consider talking to him. Basically, he's approved! "

When Momma said that, I immediately started thinking that maybe Deangelo is the right one for me. Everyone has said it. Even Latasha saw it and was trying to get his attention. Maybe I'm the one that's behind. Maybe I did need to give him a chance…

After the movie, we walked over to IHOP. It wasn't my definition of an upscale restaurant, but it was only a short distance from the movie theater. The food was good and we had a great conversation.

After a few seconds of silence, Deangelo said, "Honestly, Aaliyah, I had a great time."

I smiled. "Me too."

"And this whole…'friendly date' has really helped me realize my feelings for you. I swear, you are the girl for me. I know you wanna take things slow and I totally understand that. We've only been seriously talking for a week. But in that week, I know you're right for me right now. I don't see any more Aaliyah Andersons on the dating scene."

"Well, are you serious about us going together? One thing I don't need is any other girls taking up my guy's attention. I understand if you look, but don't touch. I've been hurt before and I don't wanna be hurt again."

"I already promised that'll never happen."

"Actions speak louder than words."

He grinned. "That's why I say we should try this relationship out. We don't have to be on some *Love & Basketball* type stuff. We can take it slow like you want to. I just know I'm feeling you and that I want to put a title on our relationship. Are you down?"

It felt like I was frozen in place! Here Deangelo was, laying it all down to me. What do I do?

I guess the only thing I could do.

I smiled at him, "Yes, Deangelo. I'm willing to make things exclusive if you are."

He smiled and reached for my hand across the table. "Trust me, Aaliyah. This is gonna work out."

"I guess we'll see…"

I can't believe I officially go out with Deangelo now! It's crazy! But one thing is for sure: I'm not gonna tell anybody yet. Maybe Allison and Dasia, because I know they won't spread it around the school, but no one else. I don't wanna jinx us. I want me and my 8/25/12 to stay together for a while (it feels so funny to say that).

So, the first part of my weekend went great. Now, I have to find a way to tell Faith that I'm her sister. After talking to Theresa, I feel a whole lot more enthusiastic about it too. I believe I really could be making a change in Faith's life. It's like my dream come true! ☺

Sincerely,

Aaliyah Anderson

Randall Barnes

Ms. Johnson

August 27, 2012, 7:43 p.m.

Saturday is officially the day that I'm going to tell Faith about our crazy family situation. I know I've been going back and forth on how and when I'll tell her ever since I learned the news, but I finally talked to her mom yesterday.

Momma invited her to the station so I could talk to her. The thing about it is that I had no idea she'd be there! It was a total shock. I was over in the studio with D. He had just gone to a commercial break and we were about to record another bumper.

Roxanne walked into the studio and said, "Aaliyah, you have somebody that's here to speak with you."

I looked to D to see if he knew if someone was coming to see me. He shrugged his shoulders. I just got up and followed Roxanne to the elevator. As we were going down, I asked her if she knew who it was down in the lobby waiting for me.

"It's Valarie Johnson, lawyer and part owner of Johnson & Wright Party Promotions. If she's here to see you with her busy schedule, it has to be important."

I immediately knew what it was for!

"I hope you're not in any legal troubles we don't know about," Roxanne teasingly said.

I smiled. "Of course not! Ms. Johnson just needs to see me for…a very important matter regarding my family."

"Is everything alright?"

"Everything's cool. It's just some things I need to get information on that I didn't know before. Do you think I could talk to you about it later? It's really complicated."

"Sure, you can catch me later on if it's convenient."

The elevator made it down to the welcome center about a minute later and I finally saw Faith's mom. They looked just alike! She stood at about 5'7" with beautiful dark brown skin and a slender yet curvy body frame. She had her hair styled in a beautiful-looking natural topknot.

"So I guess this is the Aaliyah Anderson I've been hearing so many good things about?" she asked with a smile.

Roxanne replied, "Yes ma'am, this is her. We were so proud of her at the student presidential nomination party that was held at Clarkson on Friday. She tore the house down with her speech!"

"I guess she's taking after her mother and brother, then. The amazing gift of communication runs in the family."

"It appears to be in the Andersons' DNA! But anyway, I'm going to leave you two ladies to what you planned to do. Nice seeing you again, Ms. Johnson!" Roxanne said as she walked back towards the elevator.

"Wow, it's so nice to meet you, Aaliyah," Ms. Johnson said with a bright smile.

"I say the same to you, Ms. Johnson. It was really unexpected though."

"Your mom said you'd be pretty surprised. Congratulations on your speech at Clarkson on Friday. Faith was talking about it all morning Saturday. She was extremely proud."

I smiled, feeling accomplished. "Wow! Faith was proud of me?"

"Yes! Faith thinks the world of you. The funny thing is that she's the only one that doesn't know that you're her sister. I heard you and Damon just learned about it last week."

"We did."

"How'd you feel about the news?"

We went to go sit down in the waiting area.

"I'm happy that I have a sister, but I feel guilty for how my 'father' left you and Faith behind like that. It's just not right."

"Oh, Aaliyah, you don't even have to worry about that. You had no control over what happened twelve years ago between us. All that matters is the present."

"That brings up a good question too! You said that Faith is the only one that doesn't know that we're all related, right?"

"She has no idea. I never told her because I never thought it would come up. But I believe it's time for her to know the truth."

"Exactly. So I was wondering if I could tell her. I want to do a girls' day out with her on Saturday, but I need your permission."

"That's a fantastic idea! Let me ask her about it and I'll call your Mom later on this week."

"Ms. Johnson, I've been paranoid about Faith shutting me out if I told her the news. Do you think she'll accept me after she takes in what I'm gonna tell her?"

"I believe Faith will be completely fine with you coming out as her half-sister. Trust me, I know how my baby thinks. She already looks up to you. It'll be like a dream come true if she found out you two were related. There's no reason to stress or worry."

I smiled, even more relieved. Just like that, things fell into place. Now, I still have to think and brainstorm about what I'm gonna do on Saturday to make it special and how to tell Faith. This could be more complicated than the speech!

♠♠♠♠

The Brainstorm

When I got to Momma's house, I immediately went to my room and started drawing. Last Saturday, I sketched a picture of the singer Aaliyah as an angel. I believe that's one of my best pictures I've ever done too. But this new one I made yesterday evening is by far my greatest work.

As I said, when I get my artistic flow going, I close my eyes and just draw. Yesterday, I did just that and came up with a cool, original picture of the brain. There was a red lightning bolt type line going through the middle. On the right side, I drew the sun shining bright over the top. On the left side, I drew several storm clouds with rain, lighting and hail coming from them.

With this picture, I was trying to make a statement. Sometimes, it feels as if I'm at war with myself. The right side of the brain mainly has to deal with creativity and emotion. Ever since Deangelo and I made it official and I found out that I actually do have a younger sister, my creative juices have really been flowing. I've been making sketches and drawings left and right. I've also been more happy and enthusiastic the past few days. That's the positive side of mind.

Then you have the left side, which is said to be the side that deals with knowledge and logical thinking. That's my negative side. That's where I believe all my negative, depressing thoughts come from.

"What if Faith disses you?"

"What if your relationship with Deangelo doesn't work out?"

"What if you lose this student election?"

Questions like these have been weighing down on my mind heavily over the past few days. I guess it's true that the smarter you get, the sadder you become. I've started to break down the different information that I've learned over the past week or two into negative thoughts. Ever since I learned about Faith, I've woken up straight crying my eyes out some nights. My father is a complete nobody to me but for some reason I seem to keep thinking about him and having nightmares about me telling Faith and her getting angry.

This picture was so great to me because I drew it based on what I've been experiencing. Honestly, sketching that picture really took a load off of my shoulders and stress off of my brain. It felt like I laid down all my problems on that long, white piece of construction paper. Some people smoke weed or do drugs to escape their problems. Some people use violence. I use my art. To me, that's the best self-help ever.

As I was looking over my finished product, the doorbell rang. D and I were the only ones in the house because Momma went to the grocery store. I wondered who'd be coming by at 9:23 on a Monday night?

D came out the library and went to open the door. It was Allison! When I heard her voice, I ran down the stairs and gave her a huge hug.

"Hey, Allie! What brings you down here so late?"

"I need to talk to you about some things and I couldn't seem to catch up with you. So, I heard you were in the neighborhood tonight and I decided to come down."

"Your parents let you walk down here?"

"Come on, Aaliyah! This is Brentwood! Absolutely nothing happens down here."

I smiled and said, "Okay, I'll take your word for it."

I led Allison up to my room and let her look around. She was amazed at all the new art that I had hanging on my cream-colored walls. She especially liked my pictures of Aaliyah and "The Brainstorm".

"Wow, Aaliyah! These pictures are beautiful!"

"Thanks, Allie. I've really been getting new ideas as of late."

"So this is why you haven't come down to the tennis courts once ever since you've been in Brentwood?" she asked, staring at "The Brainstorm", which was hanging up over the brown office desk that Momma got for me. Before I went down to get Allison, I pasted it on a poster board so it could look more professional. In addition to it being my best work, it's also the largest picture I've ever made.

I smiled. "Pretty much."

"Hey, you know something I just thought of?"

"What's up?"

"There's a youth art contest that my mom has been promoting at the fitness gym and her restaurant for the past week. I think you should submit your work."

I thought about it in my head for a second, "Do you think I'd win?"

Allie smiled. "Of course! Look at these pictures you drew. They're beautiful works of art that anyone can appreciate. I believe you could win first place. You know the awards for winning the whole contest are really nice."

"Explain them then."

She sat on my bed as she thought of what she heard the first place winner would receive. I still was thinking about if I should enter my work. As I've said before, I don't take criticism well. But, for what they were planning to give the overall winner of the contest, I'll just have to put on my mental bulletproof vest!

"The first place winner could get $600 in spending money, $1,500 in scholarship money for college, statewide recognition that could get people to call you to draw for money, stuff like that."

"Are you serious? When is it?"

"It's this Friday at the Art Museum downtown by Howard-Jones. Do you think you could make it?"

"Of course! Especially if you think I really have the chance to win the whole thing."

"Cool! My mom and I could pick you and the art you want to display up."

"That's fine by me."

All of a sudden, the doorbell rang again. I ran down the stairs and looked out the peephole. It was Dasia. I guess everybody in Brentwood think the same way as Allison.

I opened the door and she immediately walked in,

"What's up Aaliyah?"

"What's up, Dasia. What brings you all the way down here?"

As she was walking towards the stairs, she replied, "We have to work on this campaign! Even though Latasha's speech was lame, she's been sending more shots your way and going out to meet with different people in 8th grade to convince them to vote for her. We need to talk about what we can do to get support from the students in 6th and 7th grade. They're the most important to sway to our side because there's more of them."

I thought about what she said and nodded. "That is a good point."

"Hey, Aaliyah, I think you should---" Allison was walking down the stairs and paused in mid-sentence when she saw Dasia. She smiled, "Oh, hey Dasia!"

"What's up, Allison," Dasia replied with a smile of her own.

It's no secret that Allison and Dasia are my two best friends. Like I said before, they're more sisters to me than friends, especially Dasia.

I can come and talk to them about anything. I believe that Dasia and Allison are cool with each other, but just because they share me as a mutual friend.

When I'm around 'Kiyah, Allison tends to stay away. But, with Dasia, she'll stick around. Personally, I think they have a mini problem with each other because they each want to be the main best friend. But both of them have to co-exist together. I don't play favorites. Allison and Dasia are both number one in my book!

"It's great that both of you guys are here! I have to tell you about what happened with Deangelo. You know we go together, right?"

Both of them were surprised.

I led them to the den. "Come on and let me tell you all about what happened."

And I did just that. I told them all about what I really felt for Deangelo, how he really impressed my mom, and what happened at IHOP.

"So you two officially go together? Just like that?" Dasia asked. I nodded. She smiled. "I see what you two did. You went out to the movies as friends, but you left out IHOP friends with benefits."

"I wouldn't say 'friends with benefits', but pretty much."

Allison was excited. "I knew this would happen! Did you know that Dante and I go together now?

"Really? When did you make it official?"

"On the phone Sunday. We talked about it and decided it'll be cool if we went together."

Dasia changed the subject. "In other news: what's up with this campaign? We can talk about teenage puppy love later. What are you gonna do about Latasha re-upping her game? I overheard her dissing you pretty hard on the school news today. I think maybe it's time for you to go on D's show at Howard-Jones."

"Dasia, let me tell you just like I told Vicky on Friday: I want to win this without D's help."

"Come on, 'Liyah! You know we can't do that. Latasha's using all of her weapons, so why can't we use ours? I heard her older sister is the main producer of the television part of the journalism class at Howard-Jones. That's how she was able to get on and go a full five minutes talking bad about our campaign. We have to do something this time. Taking the high road isn't gonna help us. We need to respond!"

"I'm not snubbing D's show. I'm just saying that I'm not too quick to jump and ask D for anything regarding this campaign. We can do it without him. Let's figure out another way to get around this."

Dasia sighed and reluctantly said, "Okay, if you say so. You're the one running for student body president. I hope this doesn't come back to hurt us in the end."

After what Dasia told me, I began to start thinking again. Is she right about me needing to be more concerned about Latasha's disses towards me as a person and the campaign? Maybe I do need to plan on how to strike back. But I've gone too far to ask D for help. So far, everything has been going my way with the campaign. Personally, I think if I use the resources D has to win the election, a dark cloud would always hang over my win. I can see it now:

"Aaliyah won the first official Clarkson student presidential election, but her big brother D, who's a local sports superstar and radio personality, helped her with everything."

Can I just be independent for a change? Everybody's been hassling me to go on D's show. I'm not about to show Latasha and any of her supporters weakness. I'm gonna find a way to get back at her. Please trust that! I don't do behind-the-back talking. I'm just keeping it real. I need to do this on my own.

Sincerely,

Aaliyah Anderson

♥♥♥♥♥♥♥♥♥♥♥♥♥♥♥♥♥♥♥♥♥♥♥♥

Karen

September 3, 2012, 9:53 p.m.

My weekend started out perfectly with a great win at the Willows-field Youth Arts competition that Mrs. Pivot was sponsoring. Even with me loving art so much, I've never been to the museum before. I mean, I knew it existed, but it never really crossed my mind. Nevertheless, it's beautiful!

When they said it was an art museum, it really was an art museum. Usually, when you think of art, you instantly think of drawings, paintings, and sketches. Art is more than that and the museum really shows diversity. They even have a section of the museum highlighting popular African-American authors from the past and present along with their works. I know D would go crazy if he knew that they had that!

When Allison and I walked into the museum, I casually looked around at the other pieces that were up to be judged. I felt like my drawings weren't good enough!

"Allison, do you still think I could get first place? I mean, look at all these fantastic works of art around here. I feel seriously underprepared."

"Don't think like that, 'Liyah. Your sketches are beautiful. To me, it's the best in this room. You're just overreacting."

I nervously smiled. "Yeah, maybe that's why I'm tripping."

In actuality, I was terrified! I have no idea why I get so paranoid when the spotlight is on me. After how great I did last Friday at that nomination party, you'd think that fear would've past. Yet, we're here…

As we all were standing around waiting for the judges to start going around, a pretty dark-skinned girl with her hair styled in a Bantu knot updo came up and asked me, "Are you Aaliyah Anderson?"

I smiled. "Yeah, that's me."

She smiled back and extended her hand. "My name is Karen. I guess all I've heard about you is true. These sketches are beautiful!"

"Thanks for the compliment. I was sort of worried that they wouldn't get noticed. Compared to everything else in here, I feel like they're really plain."

"That's the same way I feel. All of a sudden, you see something that you could've changed or done better on."

"Exactly! But you have no reason to worry. Your sketch is great! You have a great concept going on. It really reminds me of *The Boondocks* cartoons."

"Wow, thanks!"

Karen, whose work was next to mine, had sketched several pictures of a black woman cartoon superhero that she called "Mrs. Independent". The really noticeable thing about her was the huge afro that she had. She had her black power thing going on! Mrs. Independent and Huey from *The Boondocks* could be related! That had to be the most unique piece of work in the competition. No one could compare to her creativity. I knew she'd get first place for sure.

After a while of talking with each other, the judges started coming around. One young female judge came up and looked at my sketch of "The Brainstorm". It looked like she was feeling it too.

"This is a really interesting piece of work. What was your motivation behind this?" she asked me.

I explained to her about the different sides of the brain and how the drawing relates to how I feel some days in my life. She was definitely impressed.

"That's very deep and enlightening. I really believe you have a chance to win this contest. This has to the most insightful work of art that I've seen all night."

My eyes lit up. "You really think so?"

"Yes! You can tell that you didn't just draw an image like everybody else. Your piece has emotion. It has a message. It's innovative. You had a great motivation for doing this piece. I'm very impressed. We're gonna see how things shape up at the end of the evening. Good work, Ms. Anderson."

My confidence was on high after she said that to me! The judge really believed I could win this thing. I overheard Karen getting a lot of love from the judges as well. It was expected though.

When the judges left and went to the other side of the crowded room full of artists, Karen turned to me and said, "Wow! I heard what she said about your drawing. She really loved it! That has to make you feel good."

"It really does. I feel like I didn't waste my time coming down here. I heard about what the judges thought about you too. All of them loved your piece."

"Yeah, I hope something comes out of it though."

I thought about how talented both of us were. If we teamed up, we could make some noise. It could be cool to finally have somebody to collaborate with and bounce ideas off of.

So I said, "You know, we would make a great team. I've never seen anyone around my age that really appreciates art the way you do."

"I feel the exact same way. We really should connect up. I heard you've been living in Brentwood with your mom."

"Yeah, but it's not official. Do you live in Brentwood?"

"Yup. I've seen you at the tennis courts with your friend over there. You two go at it for real. But I think that's a great idea. It'll be cool to collaborate with Aaliyah Anderson."

I smiled. "Why does everybody act like I'm such a big name? The only reason you know me is because D's my brother and Natasha Anderson is my mom. I feel like I'm just recognized because of the family I happen to be in."

"I wouldn't necessarily say that. I've heard people comment on how deep and lifelike your artwork is before. I've also heard about how skilled of a tennis player you are. Trust me, you're definitely not your brother or your mother's shadow."

After that, we exchanged contact information. To make it even more obvious that we should team up, we tied for first place. They gave us $300 each and a certificate.

The evening ended up very well. Mrs. Pivot took Allison, Karen, and me to her restaurant. The food was good too! Mrs. Pivot's cooks definitely know how to throw down. I felt accomplished going into Saturday, which I decided was the day that I would tell Faith about "the secret". I was still wondering how I would break it to her when

I got back to Momma's house that night. That was the only thing that was hanging over me. But no matter how I thought it would play out, I wanted closure. And that's what I got…

♠♠♠♠

The Special Moment

My day out with Faith was perfect. It was like we were celebrities! Momma got us a limo with a personal driver and everything. I wondered if Faith was getting suspicious. I mean, this was just supposed to me and her going to the mall chilling. Maybe we'd buy a few clothes. But we went and got our nails done, got massages, and then we went to the mall and got bags upon bags of clothes and shoes. It seemed like Faith was going with the flow though. That's really how her personality is. She's just a cool individual.

After we went out to eat at Chili's, I got the driver to take us to the park where I go to read and work on my art. For some reason, it's always windy down there. The park is so peaceful and tranquil. It's really a secluded place altogether. Many couples come to Riverview Park so they can be alone and talk. Some people go so they can meditate. Nevertheless, this park has to be my favorite place in the world. That's why I decided to take her here.

I took her to the table that I usually choose when I come to draw.

"Wow, this place is beautiful!" Faith said as she looked around.

I smiled. "Yup. Many people say it's heaven on earth. You can't get this type of peaceful vibe anywhere else in Willowsfield."

"Aaliyah, thank you for letting me chill with you today. We didn't even have to go out. We could've just stayed and watched TV while we talked."

"I know we sort of went over the top but it was for good reason." I hesitated and took a breath. This was the moment! "Listen, I think you should really know the truth about your family."

She turned to me. "What do you mean by the truth about my family? What's going on?"

"You know Coach Anderson, right? He's over sports and athletics at Howard-Jones."

She nodded, wondering where I was going with this.

"That's your biological father."

I could hear the pain in her voice. "So he's my father? Why hasn't he come to see me? Doesn't he know about me?"

I nodded as tears started coming out of her eyes. "Listen, Faith, all of this isn't bad news," I tried to reassure her.

"That's what it seems like to me. Why hasn't he even attempted to see his daughter? Am I not good enough for him? Why did you even tell me this?"

"Well, Faith, let me tell you the good news. I don't know if you know this or not, but Coach Anderson is our father too."

She looked up at me, knowing exactly what I was trying to say.

I was holding back tears. "All my life, I wanted a younger sister, somebody I can protect, somebody I can help and give advice to, somebody that I can forever share something with. I guess I finally got what I wanted." I continued, "Faith, I understand if you're mad at me. I just didn't want this to be a secret anymore. Ever since I've known, I've felt guilty - guilty for how that less of a man has treated you and your mother. I totally apologize."

I got up to go to the car and leave Faith alone to herself. I knew she had to be angry. She honestly took it harder than I expected. I felt horrible.

But Faith called me, "Wait, Aaliyah!"

I stopped and turned around. She ran up and hugged me, holding on to me tightly.

"Aaliyah, you don't have to apologize for anything. This isn't your fault."

"So, you're not mad at me in any way?"

She smiled at me as she wiped away her tears. "How could I be? You said that you've always wanted a younger sister. Well, I've always dreamed of having an older sibling that I can look up to. I know our dad did us all wrong, but look at the bright side. If it wasn't for him, my dream couldn't have come true. I love you, big sis."

After she said that, I couldn't hold back my tears. I hugged her back and said, "I love you too, Faith."

♠♠♠♠

Too Fast, Too Soon

I finally felt satisfied with my life after our trip to the park! The driver drove us back to Momma's house and we just chilled and talked until Ms. Johnson came to pick her up. When she left, my first instinct was to call Deangelo - my 8/25/12 ☺.

"See, didn't I tell you everything would work out?" he said in an "I told you so" type tone after I told him what happened at the park.

"You really did. The whole thing was heartwarming. I feel so complete now!"

"I bet you do. You've wanted this your whole life right?"

"I have. That's one thing I didn't lie about."

"Well, now you have your chance. You need to capitalize on it."

I smiled. "Trust me, I will."

"I believe you're gonna be the best thing to ever happen to Faith. I can just see it. You just have a giving spirit, plus you're a hustler."

"A hustler?"

"Oh, I don't mean 'hustler' as a bad thing. That's great. You're the type of girl that'll try and make money off of anything. I don't see any other females around here with drive like that. They just expect for something to be handed to them. That's the problem with our generation now."

"You know I feel the same way, right? I swear, we have no dreams or ambitions outside of the short term. We really need to tighten up."

"Exactly! You know something, 'Liyah?"

"What's up?"

"You've never told me your career goals. I've heard different things being thrown around, but I've never heard it from you. Don't you wanna be a music executive or something?"

"Not a music executive, but it's almost related. I wanna be a head of a company, whether it's mine or someone else's. I love creating, organizing, and being in charge. And I don't wanna be thirty or forty years old when I start. That's one of the two main reasons I came up with Beautiful Sistahs, Inc., so I could build up my experience."

"So what's the second reason you started your business? I know it has to be as good as the first reason."

"I believe you're gonna like this one. The overall main reason I started Beautiful Sistahs Inc. is because I wanted to assume a 'big sister' style role and help children younger than me. It was never about the money until we started getting those calls for $300 and $400 an appointment. It was always about giving a service to the community. It also was to be something that I thought I would never be until now."

"Let me guess: a big sister?"

I smiled. "Exactly."

"You know something, 'Liyah? You have a unique personality that no one else around here has. I swear, I don't know of many people around our age in Willowsfield that are worried about the well-being of the community or being the head of a company. That's why I love you. You're fine, caring, and ambitious. I thought I'd never find a girl down here down here in the 'Field like you."

I was grinning wide. "Hold up! Did you just say that you...*love* me?"

Deangelo laughed. "I believe I did. Is there a problem?"

I honestly didn't know how to take it! "It's not a problem if you really mean it. I've been told that by guys in my life countless times before and they never mean it."

"Well, I'm not one of those other guys. I know we've been only going together for a hot li'l' minute, but that's how I really feel. I've never met a girl that has what you have, Aaliyah. That's why I was so quick to lock that down. I know no other guy out here knows how to treat you like a true lady. But I know I can and I will."

I was blushing like crazy. No boy that I've talked to has ever been this straight forward with me. It's so sexy! Guys are always so heart-less and calculating when it comes to females. It's always about sex! I could tell that Deangelo was different from the beginning. I guess that's why I wasn't interested in getting with him. I wasn't used to being treated special by guys.

Deangelo broke me out of my daze by asking, "So, do you feel the same way about me?"

I'm not even gonna lie; I sort of hesitated. I mean, I do have strong feelings for him, but I don't think I can say that I love him quite yet. I honestly couldn't if I tried.

"If you don't feel the same way, I totally understand. I'm not trying to rush things if you're not."

I sighed. "Deangelo, I like you a lot but I'm not ready to say, you know, *that* yet. Don't take this the wrong way, though. You're still my boyfriend, but I don't think I'm ready to say something that extreme so soon."

"I feel you. It's totally understood."

"Going back to career goals… You've never told me yours. What do you want to do?"

"I wanna become a personal trainer, something dealing with helping people get and stay healthy. I've always been a fitness nut, even when I was a little kid. My mom swore I'd make something off of it. That's actually something I've always wanted to talk to you about."

"What, fitness?"

"Ever since I saw how driven you are, I've wanted to talk to you about starting a personal training group for teenagers that wanna get in or stay in shape. I know you have the connections to make that happen too. Plus, you could be one of the trainers."

I laughed. "You really see me as a personal trainer?"

"Of course, Ms. Tennis Superstar. If nobody else knows how to keep their body looking good, you do."

"I think it's a good idea. We could ask Allison's mom if she could give us advice and let us use her studio. She's a fitness instructor and personal trainer, you know. We could spread the word about it on HoodTalk 98.1 and even create health segment for D to do on his show."

Deangelo chuckled. "See, this is exactly why I brought it to you. You've already thought about how to make it an overnight success."

I smiled. "That's just how I am."

"So are you down with it?"

"I think we could really do that and get a lot of people to support us. We have to plan things out though. We can never go into anything without planning first. Strategy is the key."

"Alright. We can talk about it at school tomorrow."

"That's a good idea, business partner," I said with a smile.

Even though this weekend was great and very productive, I'm so glad it's over! Now I have some work to do going into the rest of the week. I have to make up for the lost time with Faith, see about this whole situation with Latasha, plan out Deangelo's idea for teenage personal fitness training while also being a good girlfriend, and still do my normal responsibilities. Plus, I wanna hook up with Karen and see what her plans are with "Ms. Independent". I think we could really do some *Boondocks* type things with her sketch...

Sincerely,

Aaliyah Anderson

❤❤❤❤❤❤❤❤❤❤❤❤❤❤❤❤❤❤❤❤❤❤❤

Willowsfield vs. Worthington

September 8, 2012, 5:23 a.m.

You know something? I've gotten tired of the stupid b.s. that goes on in the streets! Why can't we just have a period of time where nothing crazy and ratchet happens? No robbing Footlocker for the same Jordans that came out a year ago, no random shootings, no females fighting over guys that don't even care for them… I've just gotten tired of it!

Over the past week or so, Willowsfield has gotten progressively more violent. I don't know what made everybody wanna start robbing stores and fighting! We've already been going through enough in Willowsfield, but of course, there has to be even more drama.

Yesterday, I was sitting at lunch with Deangelo, Dante, and Allison. We were just talking having a good time when Tay came over, looking angry.

"What's up with you, Tay?" I asked.

"Man, did y'all see what them boys from Worthington been spreading around Facebook and Twitter? That junk is extremely disrespectful."

"Oh, you're talking about those YouTube videos dissing the city," Dante said

"Yeah, man! And the worst part is that they dissed Willowsfield specifically - not just one set or hood, thug. They tried everybody up!"

All I could do was shake my head. Worthington is a li'l' irrelevant town that's literally right next to Willowsfield. To put it plain and simple, they wanna be us. Their street life is a straight up copy of Willowsfield. They've clamed all of the major gangs that Willowsfield has except for Bernard Street. For years, they've angered a lot of gang-affiliated guys around our city, but things got super crazy after high-ranked Willowsfield Rydah member OG Rasheed posted on his Facebook as a status:

> "Rydah sh*t est. 10/25/79 Riverstone Creek
> Free BamBam and Duke
> #Rollinup"

The first thing I thought was *Duke's back in jail? Didn't he just get out?*

Then I scrolled down and started reading the comments. These guys that call themselves the "Green Hill Rydahz" started a huge argument in the comment section over whose sets were started first. I really didn't even know why I cared about this so much to sit up for an hour reading the comments. The whole situation is stupid! They're on the internet arguing over whose gang was made first. Are you serious?

The thing that was funny to me was the fact that they'd send li'l' threats after every comment, like, "*I don't be doin' all that talkin' on the 'book, thug! If you really think we fake, run up!*" or "*I don't do all this internet drama like a female. We bust shots out here, boy!*"

Really? They're over here talking about not getting into "internet drama like a female", yet they've posted 369 comments arguing with each other over Facebook about whose gang was started first. I doubt we'd even carry on some stuff on Facebook like this. Now do you see the ignorance that we have to deal with down here?

My brother Jeff even had something to say on the status. He knows he's not supposed to be on Facebook because he's on probation, but I guess he doesn't even care.

Anyways, he posted:

"Man, y'all need ta ghill with this false flaggin' b.s. If y'all swear y'all real Rydahz, learn yo set history then thug. The Rydahz were founded by Jamal Farmer, who grew up and died in Willowsfield. To keep it 100, all the gangs started down here in the 'Field. If anybody fake, it's y'all. How you gon' wear your flag to the left when you know we bang to the right down here, thug? Ghill with all that! #Eastsidelyfe #RIPOGFarmer"

Obviously, my big brother's post didn't go over too well with the "Green Hill Rydahz", so they started posting status on Facebook calling out King Street and Tweets on Twitter dissing the Killas. They even started posting videos of them in their neighborhoods talking about how fake we were and showing off their cars, guns, and drugs. Now the whole city is involved in this citywide gang war, all over one simple Facebook status. Just stupid!

"Aye, y'all know they're coming down here next Friday when Worthington High plays Howard-Jones, right? We gon' see if they really about that life!" Tay said, getting more and more hyped as he thought about the situation.

I couldn't believe what I was hearing!

"You guys are gonna start some drama at the football game over some comments on Facebook?" I asked.

"Honestly, 'Liyah, it ain't even about Facebook. It's the fact that they're trying the city up. I know you saw the post, thug. Nobody said anything about Worthington. 'Sheed wasn't even thinkin' about all that when he posted that status. He was just trying to show love to the eastside fam. But they just gonna come up trying the city like we ain't 'bout that life? Naw, man, we gon' see about them boys. I put it on my *set* we beat them too, thug."

All I could do was look at Deangelo and shake my head. I can't even go and see D play next Friday without the danger of getting shot over some Facebook drama that spilled over into the streets. Why can't we just chill out with all this craziness? I know Mrs. Conner and I don't usually see eye to eye, but what she said that first day after the "almost weed fight" is turning out to be totally true.

Worthington was straight up doing the most! They were blowing up Facebook with nonstop anti-Willowsfield statuses, comments, and posts throughout the day. They even recorded a whack rap song dissing us! Where were they finding the time to do all this? Don't they have something better to do during the day, like school or work?

The drama spilled over to HoodTalk 98.1 during MoMoney's after-noon drive show as he addressed the whole situation. Mo saw the tweets, Facebook comments, and videos about west Willowsfield and he shared his anger on the air.

"Did anybody happen to catch the latest post on Facebook from Longford Heights 'Killa' G-Dogg, a.k.a. Gerald Clark? For every-one that doesn't know, Gerald Clark is like a twenty-three-year-old, no-talent-having rapper from Worthington that's still in 12th grade. The kid lied to Worthington's school system, saying he's just twen-ty. Yeah, twenty plus three! This old man stays trying to get at these high school females too. Gerald is a straight pedophile!

"Is this cat serious, G? Is this guy *really* serious? Dude is all over Facebook and Twitter talkin' 'bout he has the rawest diss song on the 'Field ever. And I know this man couldn't be serious, G. Y'all need to hear what this dude sent out! As a matter of fact, I'ma play it later on. It's called 'Willowsfield Murderers'."

MoMoney then started laughing. "I mean…wow! They really want war with the number one most dangerous city in America? Everybody in Willowsfield just needs to chill out and let them have their shine. These boys ain't even worth the time! I mean, we made them. Everything about the 'Field, Worthington copied. They stole way we 'bang, the way we rock our gear, the way we talk, the way we spit at females. We just can't have anything to ourselves, G!

"Yo, because of FCC rules and regulations and all that, I can't send threats on the air, so I'm not even gon' get the squad in trouble, G. But Worthington's coming down to Willowsfield next week at the Jones Sport Complex. It's gonna be a good night too. D and the undefeated Howard-Jones Falcons go up against Worthington High, the high school where most of the students are older than the teachers! We gon' have the after party jumping off at Clarks & Wade Skate Center after the game. The baddest females are gonna be off in there and *ya boy* is gonna be preforming some of his songs!

"To be real, I don't even got a problem with Worthington's females, G. They got some dimes down there. Those Worthington females can get it. I have a problem with these dudes that think they gon' just diss the 'Field without getting checked. You feel me?

"I want September 14th to be a peaceful night, G. I wanna just have a smooth night with the squad and mind my own business. But if Worthington comes down here with all the disrespect, y'all know what we have to do. I'm not sending threats or anything like that. I'm just being real. Y'all know what we have to do if they come down tripping. And that's all I gotta say about the situation."

People from Worthington were extremely heated over Mo's comments. Some Green Hill Rydahz even drove down to the studio after his show was over to try and jump him.

"You took this way too far, Mo'! You're putting everybody in danger with all this!" Roxanne shouted at MoMoney. I've never seen her so angry!

Mo' shrugged it off. "Man, it's straight! I know for a fact they aren't strapped. They just down here to talk."

"The fact that they have no guns on them is irrelevant. *Your* words and actions on *your* show have led to a security problem. There's no reason for thirteen gang members to be on Carswell property waiting for you to come out so they can fight you. You better deal with this and quick, or we're gonna have a major problem."

Roxanne stormed out of the HoodTalk studios as we looked at Mo' to go out and do something.

"Man, y'all flexing! I'm not going out there to get jumped. I don't know what y'all are gonna do, but I'm out of it!"

I was stunned. "Mo, you're the reason that they're here in the first place! If you weren't running your mouth about that street b.s., none of this would even be happening! You have to do something."

He smacked his lips. "I said what I have to say, G."

I shook my head. MoMoney is supposed to be this hard body, fearless Westside Killa, but he's afraid to go resolve a problem that he's started. D had to go and get them to leave the studio grounds. He was so smooth with it, too! They didn't even fight or fuss with him. From what I saw, he just talked to them for about a minute, gave them some dap and a few autographs, and they left. MoMoney was left looking stupid.

When D came back in, Mo tried to give him some dap. He didn't extend his hand to give the love back to him. He just stared him dead in his eye and said, "Mo, this is the last time I'm gonna clean up your mess. You need to regulate what you say on the air or we're gonna have to pull your show. We can't have any more situations like this. Next time, we may not be as lucky as to run across some bangers that didn't bring their guns with them. I brought you onto this project because I'd thought you'd be perfect for the job, but I'm starting to rethink my decision. You know you're my boy and all, but whatever you do crazy makes the station look bad. This is gonna be the last time we're gonna have this conversation, right?"

Mo hesitated, then finally said, "I got you, G. I'll accept the blame. I went way overboard and it won't happen again."

D smiled and gave him some dap. "We're good now."

I admired how D handled the situation with Mo and the Green Hill Rydahz. That's how a true leader does it. That's a perfect example of how I have to be when, or if, I win the presidential election - straightforward and fearless while still levelheaded.

♠♠♠♠

An Artist's Mindset

After we left the station, I walked down to Karen's house in the front of Brentwood. It wasn't as big as the ones on our side of the neighborhood, but it looked classy and upscale. Her parents are really cool! It turns out that they are both award-winning artists. Their work was hanging all along their living room. They had a special place above the fireplace for Karen's award. It was in an all-gold picture frame that stood out from the rest of the pieces. She also has a sixteen-year-old brother, who is pretty cute and was giving me the eyes as I met their parents. He's about 6'1" with a nice swag to him but he's super skinny. It looks like he hasn't eaten in weeks! There are no muscles to be found. That is so unattractive to me!

When I walked into Karen's room, I could immediately tell that she was an artist. She had everything in her room coordinated and set up perfectly. She had sketches upon sketches hanging up in her room everywhere. Homegirl really has some talent! The thing that really surprised me is the fact that she didn't have a TV. All she had was a radio, conveniently turned to HoodTalk 98.1, and an iPhone loaded with smooth R&B and neo-soul songs.

It was fun working alongside Karen. She's a very interesting and hardworking person that's true to her art. She puts her passion for sketching over everything. That's why she said that she didn't have a TV in her room.

"It's an unwanted distraction. All TV does is make you sit on your butt all day eating and doing nothing. I have no need for it. When I'm home, I'm either reading, writing, or sketching. What's the point of watching TV for hours when you're not even benefiting from it? There's no knowledge to gain and no money for you to get - well, at least not anymore. It's just something to keep the mind of uncreative people satisfied 24/7."

Dang! I never thought of it like that! She broke it down!

"So you don't watch TV at all?"

"Every now and then when something interesting is on like *The Boondocks* or other popular shows from a few years ago, like *Lincoln Heights* and *Soul Food: The Series.* Maybe *The Game, Leverage, Hawthorne,* and *CSI.* I can watch old school shows like *The Cosby Show, A Different World, Martin, Moesha, The Proud Family,* and *That's So Raven* all day. Reality Shows make me sick to my stomach!"

"I feel the exact same way. If I wanna see grown women fighting, I can just walk down to Riverstone Creek or any other hood in Willowsfield."

"Exactly! *T.I & Tiny* is straight though. It's more like a documentary style show than a normal reality show. It really reminds me of a better, more interesting version of *Run's House* from back in the day."

"No doubt! Speaking of people fighting, did you hear about Willowsfield and Worthington?"

"Well, I heard MoMoney's rant on HoodTalk after school, but I didn't hear the whole story. What's going on?"

I let out a huge sigh. "There beefing all over Facebook and Twitter about whose gangs are real or fake. People have been saying it's gonna get violent over the next few days, especially on September 14th when Worthington High comes to play Howard-Jones. Some Green Hill Rydahz from Worthington even came down to the station to confront MoMoney after what he said."

Karen shook her head while still working on her sketch. "Do you see what I'm saying about distractions now? Instead of doing something productive or helping their communities, they fight over something so crazy and trivial! I've never understood that. Craziness like that makes me glad that I shut down my Facebook account. The only thing that I have is a Twitter and an Instagram so I can share my work with like-minded people."

"I guess you can say that's been a huge distraction for me. I've been thinking about what's gonna happen at the game next Friday all day. I was planning to just chill and watch D play while I spend time with my boyfriend, but now I have to look over my shoulder to make sure I don't catch a stray bullet."

Karen looked up from her notepad and replied, "It seems like you're scared to take the risks of life, Aaliyah. What are the odds that they'd start shooting at a high school football game that already attracts a huge number of police officers? The SWAT team may come out with this one. Nothing's gonna happen except a few of our misguided young black brothers fighting each other. It's pretty much gonna be a normal day."

I smiled. "How old are you again? That sounds like something my mom would say."

Karen laughed. "That's not the first time I've heard that question! I'm thirteen about to turn fourteen just like you. It's just that, as artists, we have to look at things in a different, more mature light."

"I feel you."

She smiled. "You've never told me about your boyfriend before. What's he like?"

"Well, we just got together, but I believe he could be the one for me. His name is Deangelo and he's so sweet! You know, not sweet like--"

Karen laughed again. "I totally understand, Aaliyah. He's caring."

"Exactly! He's different. I've never been treated like a true young woman in a relationship before. When I'm around him, he makes me feel special. I think we're gonna be together for a while."

"Wow! You don't see a lot of guys like that out now. You found you a good one."

"Are you seeing anybody?"

"I was dating this guy for a while, but we broke it off. He was a sixteen-year-old guy that goes to Jefferson that thought he could get me in the bed easy because he was older. I guess he didn't understand that I'm not one of these females out on the streets giving it out like it's about to go out of style. The crazy thing was that I thought I was in love."

"Trust me, I totally understand. Before Deangelo, my story was exactly the same. You're gonna find the guy that's right for you soon. Trust me." I then got an idea. "As a matter of fact, I think I could help you out!"

"How so?"

"Well, my homegirl hooked me up with Deangelo. I think I could do the same thing with you. You should go to the game next Friday with me."

She started back sketching in her notepad. "Football isn't really my thing."

"Come on, Karen! It's gonna be fun. It'll be a way for you to get a break from the drawing thing for a minute. Then you could meet your future man! You know you can't pass up this offer."

She looked up and smiled. "Well, if you put it like that, maybe I could go with you."

Even though Karen assures me that nothing's going to happen, I'm still sort of cautious. The guys of my generation get crazy when it comes to gangs and the streets. Just thinking about what happened at the radio station makes me wonder how far are they gonna take it? Then again, maybe I am just paranoid for some odd reason!

Sincerely,

Aaliyah Anderson

The Game

September 14, 2012 11:39 p.m.

After a long week of having to put up with all the problems in school regarding these hating teachers, hard schoolwork, and this annoying student election, I thought I could get a cool night for the game. I thought I could have a good time with my friends and go to the after party at the skate center with no problems or incidents. I deserved a good time after all I've had to put up with over the past two weeks!

Once again, I thought wrong…

The game wasn't lame at all and I really did have a good time with Deangelo, Allison, Tay, Dante, and Karen. We just had to deal with so much drama that it took away from the experience.

For example, the game hadn't even started and a few Rydahz from Willowsfield were about to start fighting with some of the members of Worthington High's football team. As we were sitting on the bleachers waiting for the game to start, some girls from Worthington High were giving Jay the eye like they were interested. At first, he didn't notice it, but Polo made sure he caught on.

"Aye Jay, those girls over there choosin' up on you pretty hard."

"Where at, thug?"

Polo motioned towards the football field at two redbone girls that looked like they'd let the whole football team get some action. They were matching, wearing too-tight multi-colored leggings with jean jackets over tight, clean white wife beaters that barely covered their breasts. It looked like they were about to walk down Lakeview Avenue on the southside, the main "hoe" stroll in Willowsfield. I have no idea why guys are so naturally drawn to jump-offs! Stevie Wonder could see that they were nobody to mess with!

I looked at them a li'l' bit closer and figured out that they were from Worthington. People from Willowsfield have a certain look and swag to them that those two jump-offs didn't possess.

Polo and Jay were about to go over and talk to them when I said, "You guys know they're from Worthington, right?"

Polo looked a li'l' bit closer at them and could tell the same thing. "'Liyah's got a point. They definitely don't look like they're from the 'Field."

"Man, I don't even care. None of them boys can beat me, so I'm straight. You feel me?"

Jay smacked Polo in the chest. "You still down for the double team, thug?"

Polo laughed. "What type of question is that? You already know I'm down! Just let me talk to the baddest one."

"Does it really matter? Both of 'em look good."

I just shook my head. The love of these "hoes" really is the downfall of young men everywhere!

They talked to the girls for about two minutes and got their numbers without any problems. I thought I was just overreacting again - that is, until a few minutes later when Polo went back to the Falcon's locker room. Jay and I were just sitting talking about some things when three huge Worthington High Football players came up to him.

"I heard you were trying to spit at my girl."

Jay semi-arrogantly replied, "I wasn't *tryin'* to spit; I *was* spittin' at your girl. If you were doing her right, maybe she wouldn't have come over to see me, thug. Your girl was choosin' up on a thug hard."

The guy looked heated. Jay wasn't intimidated in the slightest.

"You think you're funny, huh? We ain't even tryin' to play with you fake Willowsfield bangers. You better keep yo' eyes off my girl before we drop you."

Jay immediately hopped up. "What's good then?"

I mean, Jay is a good fighter and everything, but I think he would've had a few problems with these two huge boys that dude brought with him. The guy he was getting into it with had some size on him too. Jay didn't back down though, which is something I always admired about him. He isn't scared of anything or anyone.

Help came for Jay quickly though as Jeff, Elijah, and these three other Rydahz nicknamed Braids, Smoke, and QT came down to even the odds. I rolled my eyes as Jeff talked all types of trash.

"All that jumpin' b.s. ain't goin' down tonight, thug. You're in the 'Field now. We hit one-on-one down here, thug."

When the other Rydahz came over to help Jay, ol' dude who was acting all hard immediately toned down all his talking. It was really funny to me! When they stacked up on him, he already knew what time it was.

Before things got out of hand, the coaches for Worthington High broke the guys up. When they left, Jeff did the Rydah gang handshake with Jay.

"You straight, thug?" he asked Jay.

"Yeah, Eight. Those boys didn't want it."

"What they came ova' here for?"

Jay smacked his lips. "They were hurt over some girl that was choosin' up on me, thug. Just some female junk, really."

"We handled that though. On the set we were gonna smash them. They knew it too."

They did the Rydah handshake again and I just stared at Jeff. He didn't even acknowledge me, which really made me angry. I am his sister, after all. I stopped getting sad about it a while ago. It really just makes me mad now. What did I do to make him hate me so much? Whatever. I can't worry about b.s. that I can't change.

On a positive, surprising note though, Elijah actually spoke to me. After Jeff and the other Rydahz he brought with him went on about their business, we talked for a few minutes. I asked him if he wanted to chill with me one day soon and he said yes. I'm trying my absolute best to make strides in repairing my relationship with him. Hopefully he was serious about his answer.

Anyway, that was one drama-filled situation out of like twenty others tonight. Things got even worse, especially when the game started. Willowsfield vs. Worthington became more than a simple street beef. It turned into a full-out city war!

Karen & Tay

Karen and Deangelo arrived at the game a few minutes before kickoff. Everything was delayed because the players were already trying to get into it with each other.

"What's up, Aaliyah? Did I miss anything?"

I shook my head. "Nothing but arguments. There's already been like four confrontations and the game hasn't even started yet."

"Is this whole city beef that serious?"

I shrugged my shoulders. "I guess it is to all the street guys."

A few seconds later, Deangelo and Tay walked over. I immediately introduced Deangelo and Karen to each other. They shook each other's hands.

"I've heard a lot about you, Deangelo," Karen said with a huge, bright grin.

"Good things, I hope," Deangelo teasingly said.

"Oh, no doubt!" she said while looking at me with a sly smile.

Out of the side of my eye, I caught Tay checking out Karen. She *was* looking cute tonight with a tan jacket over a white blouse with light blue fitted Levi jeans and tan Sperrys. Her hair was styled into an afro similar to how Erykah Badu wears hers. Because of that fact, I decided to just pretend like I didn't see it, but then Tay walked up on the side of me.

"Aye, 'Liyah, can I talk to you for a second?"

We walked over a few steps from Deangelo and Karen. "Sure, what's up?"

"What's up with yo' girl? She's all types of fine."

I folded my arms. "Yeah, Karen's real cool."

"You think you could put me up on her?"

I looked at him with that stare that stare that meant. "Are you serious?" Tay had said it himself; he's a player. He runs through females quick, especially if they're aren't getting with the sex program. Karen just got out of a bad relationship too. Why, in my right mind, would I hook them up? I said I'd hook her up with somebody good, not someone that'll break her heart even more!

"I don't think you two would work out."

"Why you say that?"

"Because you two are total opposites. Nope, you two definitely wouldn't work out."

"And how do you know that?"

"Because I know you, 'playa'! I know for a fact you're not trying to settle down. I also know for a fact you aren't trying to get with a girl like Karen. She's a true young woman. She isn't giving it up quick like the females you're used to either."

"Well dang, 'Liyah! Can I change, thug? I done got tired of all the fakes out here. I'm tryin' to wife a real female up for a change."

I looked him in the eye. "Are you serious?"

He patted himself in the chest. "I put it on the set, thug."

I thought about it, then said, "Alright, but if she doesn't like you, don't get mad at me. I tried my best!"

Tay smiled cockily. "I got that on lock, thug. Just put me up on her."

"You gotta stop all that 'on the set', 'yeah, thug' Rydah type stuff too. That's gonna totally turn her off. Remember, you're not talking to the regular jump-off on the streets."

"Alright, I got you."

So we turned around and walked over to Karen. Before we did that, though, he pulled his slightly saggin' Levis up, brushed his hair, and put on some Carmax. I just chuckled and shook my head.

Karen and Deangelo were sitting down small-talking when I said, "Pardon me for interrupting your conversation, Karen, but I forgot to introduce you to one of our *close* friends. His name is Taylor and he goes to Clarkson with us."

She grinned wide and said, "Wow! It's so nice to meet you Taylor."

He smiled wide and rubbed his hands together. "Everybody calls me Tay for short."

Deangelo looked at him and said, "You know, I was just talking to Karen and she informed me that she's an artist."

Tay put his hands in his pocket and said, "Okay, that's what's up. I've actually wanted to learn how to get my drawing skills on point for the longest time."

Her eyes widened and she smiled. "Really? You're an aspiring artist?"

"Well, I wouldn't say I'm an artist quite yet, but I have the ambition to get up there one day. The only thing I can accurately draw right now is some stick figures."

She laughed. I have to give it to Tay. With the help of Deangelo, who obviously mentioned the fact that Karen was an artist on purpose, he was able to build up a rapport with her. It was totally unexpected how much of a connection they had! They eventually exchanged numbers and were talking the whole game. Tay was so involved with getting to know Karen that he didn't even fight in the huge Willowsfield-Worthington riot after the game.

I'm getting ahead of myself, though…

♠♠♠♠

Total Disrespect

After the first quarter, Howard-Jones was winning the game 14-10. D got one of the touchdowns with an impressive drive from the forty yard line. The stadium was going crazy when he made it to the end zone. You couldn't hear anything!

Worthington was making it a good game though. Their QB Jason Dawkins has some skill. He got the first touchdown of the game, breaking tackles like a running back. Polo was heated because he felt like he was the reason why he got to the end zone so easily.

The attention quickly turned from the football game to the stands when the guys from Worthington, headed by G-Dog, started disrespecting all the sets from Willowsfield by shouting disrespectful words and throwing down their gang signs.

"Aye, do y'all see what they're doing?" Wyatt asked Jay and Jeff. After moving around the whole quarter, they were now sitting behind us.

"Yeah, thug. Those boys are disrespectful! We got them after the game though," Jay calmly said, shaking his head.

Jeff smacked his lips. "Forget all that, thug! We need to deal with that now! You know what I mean?"

They all agreed and Jeff got about thirty-three other Rydahz who were ready to go over to Worthington's side and start some major drama.

Allison pulled Wyatt by the arm before he started following behind the other Rydahz. "What are you about to go do?'

"We're about to deal with these Worthington boys disrespecting the city."

Allison shook her head. "Are you serious, Wyatt? You're about to go over and start a fight over something as stupid as them dropping some gang signs?"

"You don't even understand, li'l sis."

"No, I understand perfectly. You aren't even in a gang! You really need to sit down somewhere."

Wyatt looked at her like she was crazy, jerked his arm away forcefully, and caught up with the rest of the Rydahz. She was distraught.

Dante hugged her. "Don't trip about all that, bae. You can't control what he does."

"I know, but he should have enough common sense to not get involved with things that don't even concern him."

I said to Allison, "Nothing's gonna happen, Allie. Just look."

I pointed at the huge group of Rydahz that were going over to Worthington's side and being stopped by members of the Willowsfield SWAT team. Karen's prediction was right. They were strapped like they were going to war too. I'm not playing either. It looked like they had military weapons! The Rydahz immediately turned around and the guys from Worthington were calling them all types of fake and scary.

I turned to Tay and Karen. They were still over there flirting. I expected Tay to be one of the guys walking over to try and fight. I smiled to myself. Maybe Tay really is good for her. I admit when I'm wrong!

Allison was still angry. From what Allison told me later on, Wyatt's been trying to get into the streets something hard. He seriously wants to be ghetto! Wyatt's even been getting in a lot of trouble at Jefferson running with the Rydahz down there. Allie has been really worried that he's going down the wrong path as of late.

I'ma say it like Esquire did in my favorite movie *ATL* when he found out Lauren London's character New New wasn't from the hood and was the daughter of wealthy businessman John Garnett.

"You can have the piss in the hallway. I'll take the Picasso!"

This hood life isn't what it's cracked up to be. Trust me, I've been there! There's nothing glamorous about being ghetto or ratchet. I wish, for Allison sake, that Wyatt gets that through his head before it's too late, because after what happened at the end of the game, it seems life things are starting to get real!

But, once again, I'm getting completely ahead of myself…

♠♠♠♠

The Riot

In the end, Worthington High got destroyed by the undefeated How-ard-Jones Falcons 41-17. D got five touchdowns and had the crowd going crazy the whole game. Worthington was distraught as Wil-lowsfield celebrated over the murder that was just preformed. That's what really sparked off the problems.

As everybody ran on the field, the Willowsfield Rydahz were all together in one huge group. I guess they were getting ready for something to pop off. I was trying to find D so Karen could meet him. I wanted to introduce them because D said that he could help us with writing a storyline for the comic strip that we were planning to do with Karen's character Ms. Independent. I told you that we're trying to do *Boondocks* type stuff with this project!

All of a sudden, the huge group Rydahz and players from Worthing-ton High's football team started fighting out of nowhere. Some Worthington gangbangers made their way over to Howard-Jones's side and sparked a few confrontations. After that, everybody just started fighting around the stadium. Even the police officers were involved. It was crazy! Chairs and tables were getting thrown, people were getting knocked over and knocked out. The Jones Sports Complex was in total chaos!

Wyatt was fighting with a Worthington High football player on the field as Allison was trying to pull him back.

"Come on, Wyatt! We need to get out of here!"

Wyatt started swinging at the guy and it threw Allison off balance. She fell on the ground hard.

We ran over to see if she was okay. Allie was crying like crazy.

"Wyatt's gonna be okay, Allie. We gotta go."

"I'm not leaving without him!" Allison shouted as tears ran down her face. I tried to pick her up off the ground, but she was making it hard with all the unnecessary movements she was making.

On the first row in the stands, Jay had just laid out a skinny Green Hill Rydah as another one was about to creep up on him and clock him with a folding chair.

I shouted, "Look out, Jay!"

However, before dude with the chair could even make a move, two Willowsfield Killas pushed him up against the wall and jumped him out of nowhere. I was amazed! Even Jay was surprised. When it comes to fighting for city pride, we can stand together, but not for anything else. That's a major problem that we need to deal with!

Deangelo and Dante made their way through the crowd of people running for the exits. Dante looked at Allison. Her eyes and face were completely red and her hair was messed up.

"What happened? Why she crying like this?"

I shook my head. "Wyatt decided to fight in the riot and Allie is upset. He mistakenly pushed her on the ground too."

Dante went to calm her down.

Deangelo came up to me and said, "Dante and I have been looking all over for you guys. Are you alright?"

"I'm good. Where's Karen?"

"With Tay. He said he and his big brother would take her to her house. I called your mom and told her what happened. She said she was coming as fast as she could."

I just shook my head and pulled my phone out of my Gucci handbag.

"Boy, this has been a day!"

I dialed D's number. D picked up within a matter of seconds.

"Hey, Liyah. Are you okay?"

"I'm good - just a li'l shaken up, but I'm good. Where are you?"

"We're in the locker room with Coach Turner and some of the other football players. He told us to stay in here so there won't be any trouble concerning us, but Jeff got a few of the other gang-affiliated Rydah guys and snuck out."

"Momma's coming to get us. You need to meet us---"

All of a sudden, somebody let off five shots in the parking lot. If things weren't crazy enough!

"They're shooting outside too?"

"Yeah, it just started, but…D, we gotta get outta here!"

"Alright. Polo, Sean, and I are coming out now. Make sure you tell Moms to come through the back so she won't get caught up in whatever's going on in the main parking lot."

"Okay, D. I'll tell her."

♠♠♠♠

The Aftermath

We managed to make it back to Brentwood with no problems. Things downtown got hectic though. They were shooting and fighting down at Clarks & Wade Skate Center too! The after party was officially canceled as the police and Willowsfield SWAT team swarmed the area and started making arrests. They managed to catch the guy that started shooting in the parking lot at Howard-Jones quickly. He was a seventeen-year-old Green Hill Rydah. They showed his picture on the news. He looked like something was majorly wrong with him!

Deangelo's mom came and got him, Dante, and Allison. We dropped Polo and Sean off at their respective houses. When I was done calming myself down, I called Karen to check on her. She was perfectly fine. When Deangelo told me that Tay was going to "take her home", I immediately got worried and wonder what he meant by that. Fortunately, he actually took her home. Karen then thanked me for hooking them up and told me how much of a gentleman he was. I just listened, wondering how long that'll last.

I'm not trying to think low of Tay. I just really believe he can't handle a girl as mature as Karen at this point. It seemed to have worked out for tonight, but how long will it last? I guess time will tell on that one…

After I hung up with Karen, I called Faith. She was blowing up my phone like crazy! Faith sent me nineteen text messages and called me six times. I know she was worried about me, but dang!

"What's up, Faith?"

I heard her let out a sigh. "You're okay! I swear I've been worried ever since I heard about the Rydahz that tried to go over and confront the guys from Worthington after the first quarter. I also heard a girl got hit by a stray bullet in the parking lot and I was scared by the possibility that it could be you. They didn't give much information on here and I let my imagination go crazy. Why didn't you reply back to my texts?"

"I had my phone on silent. I was with Deangelo and I didn't want anything to distract us from our time together."

"Well, I'm just glad to see that you're still alive after all that craziness! What happened?"

"You already know what the deal is. They took this whole entire city beef too far. I understand a li'l' rivalry, but all this drama was uncalled for."

"Who won the game?"

"Howard-Jones won 41-17. D got five touchdowns."

"Whoa! That could be why Worthington was mad. They were embarrassed!"

"Yeah, but that doesn't give them a reason to start a riot! The situation on Facebook isn't either. You know the craziest part of the whole entire situation though?

"What?"

I shook my head. "The fact that everybody from Willowsfield stood together for a change. No matter what gang the guys were a part of, they fought together! Why can't we come together more often and for better causes than to fight each other? Why can't we go to war against these racist white gangs like the KKK and the skinheads instead of another majority black city? That was just something I was thinking about."

Faith replied, "That's a good point too, but you already know how things are nowadays. They'll only get along for something as crazy, ghetto, and ratchet as fighting and shooting over Facebook drama. We really need to change the way we think. Maybe if we did, crazy things like this won't happen so often."

What Faith said made me smile. It's funny how we have the same thoughts on things. It's good to see that I'm not the only person that thinks intelligently. It's even better to know that I have a sister that thinks and acts intelligently. ☺

I've gotten completely tired of the behavior of people in this city. I've gotten tired of the behavior of people in general to be honest. As I asked before, why can't we just have a period where nothing crazy happens? Why can't we just live peacefully with each other without any drama? Here's an even better question: why is my black community so messed up and what can we do to change what's going on?

Sincerely,

Aaliyah Anderson

Unexpected Change

September 22, 2012 11:25 p.m.

Life is good, life is good! Things have been going so much better in my life the past week. I swear it feels as if I have a natural high, no drugs needed. It feels like I'm at the top of the world!

I finally convinced Momma to let D and me move in with her. After the whole drama with Willowsfield and Worthington died off, we started back living in our "father's" house in Hillsdale. I went from feeling great to miserable in a matter of one day. When I'm in my "father's" house, I feel like a prisoner to the problems that he's caused in my life. Faith can't possibly come over and chill with me when I'm at his house. How would that look?

Then, I feel like I'm a prisoner to my older brother Jeff's scorn and hatred. You should just see how he looks at me - if he even looks at me at all. It really hurts! Elijah and I have been on good terms lately, but it still pains me to see him come in and out of the house high and drunk out his mind. I *still* feel like I'm responsible for his downfall.

It got to the point where I couldn't take being around that house much longer and I had a talk with D about it. It was September 17th and we were watching the Falcons beat up on the Broncos on ESPN. D was in a good mood because the Falcons were his favorite football team and they were doing really well. Matt Ryan had just thrown a touchdown pass to Roddy White, which was the only touchdown of the third quarter.

When the game went to commercial break, I asked D, "How do you feel about living down in Brentwood on a daily basis?"

D shrugged his shoulders and took a sip of his ice cold green Powerade. "I mean, it doesn't matter to me. I'm straight anywhere. What makes you ask that?"

I smiled. "No reason."

He laughed. "Okay, I'll just act like I don't care until you tell me."

"You really wanna know?"

"Of course I do."

I sighed and expressed what I was feeling to him. I didn't leave anything out either.

He shook his head and asked me, "You've really been feeling like this the past few days?"

"Yes! Just being here is really stressing to me. I just feel so dirty living here with him while Faith has never even spoken to him."

"Well, why haven't you talked to Moms about this yet?"

"I'm afraid she'd say no or prolong her answer again."

"I see what you're saying. Listen, after the game, call her and tell her how you feel. I swear, she'll let us stay down there."

So I waited until the game was over and went to my room to call her. We talked for about a minute as I told her how I felt and asked the question that's been burning inside of me for the past few days.

Her answer was short and simple. "Yes, you two can. If I knew it was that much of problem to be around his house, I wouldn't have had you go back."

I was so excited! It was the most satisfied I've felt since I told Faith that we were sisters a while back. It's amazing living in Brentwood. It's so peaceful and tranquil on our street. Instead of going to Riverdale Park all the time, I now can just sit on the porch to read, write, and draw.

Practically everybody I'm cool with lives down here. My homegirl Jazmine, Allison, Dasia, Karen, Faith, Polo, Victoria, Lyric, and even Deangelo! Speaking of Deangelo, the move really helped in jumpstarting our mini teenage personal training business. I'm now closer to Allison's mom's studio and the recreation center so it's easier to serve our client'. We've been pretty successful too. "Street Fitness" officially started September 19th and we're already attracting a lot of members to our team.

♠♠♠♠

The Willowsfield Community Service Day

Earlier today at Wimberley College, we participated in their Community Service day. Every third Saturday in September and January, students of the college and select groups of people from different middle and high schools go out into the Willowsfield community to clean up and learn how to better service the city. Ever since my Auntie Vanessa started this event four years ago, it's been a major hit. However, with Momma being the executive director of the event this year, she promised at the meeting yesterday that this one would be the best that we've ever produced and the start of a major change in the whole entire concept of the community service day.

Momma addressed the college students, various community leaders, and sponsors that attended the meeting about the new changes that were coming. "Usually we feed everybody breakfast, send them off to do their few hours of service in the community, bring them back and give them lunch then send everybody home. That's so boring and uneventful! We need to make this day more interesting and important so we *know* that everybody is working to the best of their abilities."

Ever since she gave that li'l' teaser of what was to come, I was trying to get her to tell me. I know I was being nosy, but I really wanted to know what she was talking about! As we were driving back to the house after the meeting, I finally thought I'd broken her down. But all she did was look over at me, smile, and say, "You'll see tomorrow. You'll be surprised, I promise. Good things come to people who wait."

Knowing how Momma thinks, I knew whatever she planned would be big. Honestly, I couldn't go to sleep because I was thinking about what the day would be like. I didn't go to sleep at all! I just stayed up reading and working on my drawings until my iPhone alarm rang at 4:30.

That's one thing that about the community service day that really annoys me. You have to wake up super early just to get there on time. It took me about forty-five minutes to do my daily morning routine. I put on my light blue Levi jean jacket over my white Polo shirt with the matching 511 jeans and some white and blue Jordan

7's. I know we're supposed to be working today, but I have to look good!

Momma told me if I woke up early, it was my job to wake up everybody else and make sure they were ready to go at six o'clock. She was already down at Wimberley College getting things prepared. I knew for a fact that D was already up, so I went to Faith's room first. Momma also let Faith and Dasia stay over for the night. She said they could sleep over if they promised they'd work hard when it was time for them to do so.

It took me forever to wake Faith up! She sleeps peacefully, but very hard. I know it took me a good four minutes! I had to tickle her until she popped up out of bed.

"Okay, okay! I'm up!" she shouted out with a huge grin on her face.

I then went to wake up Dasia with no problem. We were all ready by 5:25 when Momma came to pick us up.

♠♠♠♠

Auntie 'Nessa

No matter how many times I visit Wimberley, I still can't believe that they haven't rebuilt the campus yet. It's like when you enter the college grounds, you go back in time to the 1800's. The building that Auntie 'Nessa's office is in looks like a plantation! I mean, seriously! It's just one huge building with a long, lengthy field.

We immediately drove to the Oliver Tombs student center where the lunchroom was located. That's where Momma and Auntie 'Nessa decided to set up the headquarters for the whole community service day. When we walked in we saw that Polo's sister Jalia was among the several other people waiting to be told what to do and where to go. My Auntie Vanessa was at the doorway making sure everything was going smoothly and running on time. Polo, Jamarcus, and Uncle Thomas were lifting and bringing in all the stuff from the outside that was for the community service day. D went out to help them.

"I know that's not Aaliyah coming in, looking like a twin version of your Momma!" she said as I went over to give her a hug.

"How's everything going, Auntie?"

"For one thing, I'm tired! I went from teaching six straight periods of English and Afro-American Literature to immediately putting the finishing touches on this community service day. But it's well worth it for all we have planned."

I cracked a grin. "Do you think you could fill me in on what you guys have planned?"

She smiled and put her hands on her hips. "Don't even try it, 'Liyah. Your Momma told me *specifically* to not tell you anything."

I laughed and shrugged my shoulders. "Well, it was worth a try!"

One thing I've always admired about Auntie 'Nessa is that she's such a hard worker. If being a college professor is hard work, you wouldn't be able to tell it by looking at my auntie. She makes teaching two of the most major subjects at Wimberley College look effortless. Her students love her for her energetic and humorous teaching style. She makes her classes fun! Aunt Vanessa is my mom's younger sister, but you wouldn't be able to tell. She's has a strong, vibrant personality that commands attention whenever she walks in a room.

Another thing about Auntie 'Nessa is that she always reps Sigma Beta. She *loves* her sorority! She was even repping for the Sigs at the community service day. Auntie Nessa was wearing a white and purple Sigma Beta graphic T-shirt, slightly loose-fitting cargo shorts, and white Nike Air Max 90's.

One thing I don't understand about my auntie is how she has continued to work at Wimberley College for four years, though. These white folks down there are super racist! Auntie 'Nessa could get a job at Willowsfield University easily, with or without Momma being on the board of directors. She has degrees in English, Literature, and History, a master's degree in Business Administration, and she is working extremely hard to get her doctorate. But the people at Wimberley still treat her like she's barely a step above being a janitor.

Then again, the janitors probably have gotten a raise in the past three years. For all the hard work and positive exposure she brings Wimberley, all she gets in return is drama and complaints. I just don't understand why she allows herself to go through this on a daily basis.

After talking with Auntie 'Nessa, Faith and I walked back to the booth where D, Polo, and Jalia were sitting. Jalia was on her phone and Polo was reading a book. Faith and I were shocked because we never knew Polo to be an avid reader like us. He usually has the same mindset that Theresa had when it came to books.

"What's going on, Polo? Since when have you started reading books?" I asked after I gave Jalia a hug.

He cracked a grin. "What are you trying to say, 'Liyah?"

I smiled. "I'm saying it's *extremely* rare to see you reading a book."

Jalia laughed. "Hey, 'Liyah does have a point."

He smacked his lips and smiled. "Man, whatever! I read, but it's hard to find books that pique my many interests, you know what I mean? This book that 'Marcus passed along to me earlier is nice though!"

He closed the book and turned it around to the cover. I smiled when I saw the title of the book. He was reading a book called *The Mack Within* by Tariq Nasheed. I knew he had to be reading a book about relationships!

"Aye, I've heard of him. Didn't he make that movie called *Hidden Colors* that we went to go see last year in Atlanta?" D asked.

"Yes! He's spitting straight up game in this too! He talks about how to analyze the personality of a female and change your game up to match their attitude. I swear, this dude is the truth!"

I rolled my eyes, folded my arms, and smiled. "You really think that a book that small can help you understand the way we act and think?"

"See 'Liyah, you got it all twisted! It ain't even about how to understand females. It's about how you can unlock the true mack that's inside of you. You really should stop judging it by the title and get up on this game! Tariq makes books for women too. You should get *Play or Be Played*, his first book that he published for females. From what I heard, he's tries to put y'all up on some knowledge too."

Jalia smacked her lips. "Boy, you know you need to quit! You know you're not a player, mack, or whatever."

"See, Jalia knows she's trippin' because she knows I'm true to the game. On life, all of her sophomore friends stay tryin' to talk to me and I don't even mess with them like that! I'm just doing me."

We all laughed at what he said. Polo does have a point though. He has the girls around Willowsfield going crazy without even trying all that hard. I may try to see if I can get that *Play or Be Played* book he was talking about. Considering my luck with relationships before Deangelo, maybe a different perspective wouldn't hurt. Besides, if this guy has Polo reading his stuff and saying it's legit, he has to be doing something right!

D smiled and said, "You guys keep trying Polo about his reading, but it doesn't even matter as long as he gets *my* book. He may never read again, but as long as he reads and enjoys *my* book, it wouldn't even matter to me!"

We all laughed again. Polo gave D some dap and said, "You already know I got you, D."

♠♠♠♠

Crystal

I was so excited to see my cousin Crystal, who's a freshman at Willowsfield University. She's the only daughter of my police officer uncle Lance Smith and a major role model for me. Crystal has successfully made it to the point where I want to be. She was the class president last year at Howard-Jones and led the protests against the Willowsfield school board for the crazy new policies that they were trying to put into action a little bit over a year ago. Crystal was named the class valedictorian and had one of the highest GPA's and SAT scores that the district had ever seen.

Of course, that allowed her attracted a lot of scholarship offers from big name colleges around the country, but she chose to stay in her home city and go to Willowsfield University to continue her push to becoming an engineer. When she walked into the lunchroom, I immediately went over so I could hear everything about her experience so far in college. I wanted to know every exact detail, from her classes to the different people that she's met on the campus!

I got Faith to come so I could introduce them to each other. She wasn't saying much of anything to anybody except me until Theresa and her family came later on.

"So Crystal, from the looks of it, it seems like you're about to pledge Sigma Beta!" I said with a smile.

Crystal, who could go for Keke Palmer's twin, had on the exact same Sigma Beta graphic T-shirt that Auntie 'Nessa had with some light blue jeans and white and purple Adidas Superstars. She was even rocking a nice-looking purple and yellow Sigma Beta snapback turned backwards.

"Oh, I just put this outfit on because Auntie 'Nessa and the other Sigma Beta girls begged me to. It's nothing major."

"Are you about to join?"

She shrugged her shoulders. "I guess I'm leaning towards it. All these sororities want me to become a member, and it's really a hard choice. They take this Greek life thing to another level. These different fraternities and sororities even have beef with each other. It goes beyond just stepping too! There was almost a huge fight at the Omega's step show dealing with the AKA's and Sigma's. I swear, they treat their respective organizations almost like gangs."

I was stunned. "Are you serious?"

"I'm for real! This isn't the same Greek scene that Auntie Natasha, Roxanne Steele, and Brianna Carter were a part of back in the day - you know, where everyone used to be cool no matter what frat or sorority you pledged. That's definitely not the case anymore, at least not down here at this university. Things have changed! The whole entire *Stomp the Yard* movie series is starting to seem a little bit more like fact than fiction."

"Wow! It seems like people from Willowsfield always take things too far. They found a way to make college crazy and ghetto!"

"I'm telling you! But college life is still good. It's cool not having to have your parents all on your case 24/7. You're responsible for yourself." She grinned. "But enough about me! What's up with you, 'Liyah? I heard a few things about you."

I smiled. "Like what?"

"Like you doing it big at Clarkson. I heard you were running for student body president, just like your big cousin. I guess I finally have someone to follow in my footsteps, huh?"

I looked at Faith and grinned. "I guess you do! But it's been rough dealing with all these hating people trying to bring me down. I told you about Latasha, right?"

"More times than I can count! Is she that much of a problem?"

"Yes, Crystal! You can ask Faith about her. She's gonna wind up winning too. She's been gathering a lot more support from the 8th graders than I have, plus all the older teachers are on her side and hate me."

"You're worrying too much about the negatives. From what I heard, you aren't doing all that bad! It seems as if Latasha is just throwing up her party and field trip ideas while disregarding everything else. Yeah, that may appeal to the ignorant, uncivilized mass of 8th graders that are at Clarkson, but you don't need their support anyway. Remember, a true student body president is the sole representation of what the school stands for and has to offer. I mean, who'd be a better representative of Clarkson than you? You're a future company CEO!"

"So you think I should keep my school improvement vibe going?"

"Of course! Don't switch up your plans because those 8th graders aren't listening to what you have to offer. They're just one li'l' part of the school population. Who you really need to get on your side is the underclassmen and the younger teachers. Has Latasha been talking to them?"

I shook my head. Crystal smiled and said, "See, there you go! All you have to do is get them to support you and the race is as sure as won. No stress or anything!"

"You're completely right! I didn't think about it like that. Thanks, Crystal!"

"That's what I'm here for, 'Liyah. I guess you've forgotten that since you haven't been calling or texting me like you used to."

I nervously smiled. "My bad! I'll make sure to hit you up on a more daily basis."

I have no idea why I didn't think to talk to Crystal about my problems in the election. She is experienced in this, after all! Both Latasha and I had been disregarding the 6th and 7th graders. Latasha's been too busy throwing shots my way and I've had a lot of stuff to deal with in my personal life recently alongside my campaign. Nevertheless, they were the real keys to the election because there's more of them than us. I need to keep that in mind because that's too big to just dismiss!

 "What's up with you, Faith? You've been quiet this whole entire time," Crystal asked her.

Faith nervously grinned. "I'm just listening and learning. I'm not trying to interrupt your conversation."

I smiled and said, "Faith is just a little bit shy, especially when she goes to new places."

Crystal nodded. "I totally understand! Aaliyah has told me a lot about you, including how good of a cheerleader you are."

"I do alright," she humbly replied.

"Faith is about the best on the whole squad, regardless of grade," I said for her.

Crystal smiled. "That's what's up! If you keep that up, you're gonna have these sororities going crazy trying to get you to step for them when you get to college."

Faith and Crystal engaged in conversation about college and I just sat there and listened. It felt so special to see them interacting with each other.

♠♠♠♠

Pendleton Homes

One of Momma's revolutionary new ideas for the community service day was to make it a competition. Every group of college and high school students who signed up to be a part of the event was put into groups personally selected by Momma and the other community leaders who were sponsoring us. Whoever worked the hardest and did the most service, according to the community leaders who would be keeping an eye on everything, would get the first place prize of a huge gold trophy and prizes that included a brand new Kindle Fire, a

$200 Visa gift card, a $250 Hollister gift card, and a free pass to all the step shows that the campus will be held at Willowsfield University.

And that was only the first surprise…

Everyone immediately got competitive. There was a lot on the line this year. People couldn't just go and not work like they did on previous community service days. Nope, this time money was involved, and money will motivate people do anything!

I had pretty much a perfect team. I was in a group of about twenty-four people and most of us were athletes. You had D, Wyatt, Jay, Blaze, Polo, 'Marcus, Deangelo, Sean, and a standout senior Howard-Jones basketball player that D's cool with named Keith Reese, just to name a few of the guys that I actually knew. Then, on the female side of things, you had me, Allison, Lyric, Victoria, Faith, Dasia, Theresa, Crystal, and a few Sigma Beta girls from Willowsfield University.

We were sent to go to Pendleton Homes, a housing project located on the west side of the city where Momma does one of her many afterschool and mentor projects. It's one of the poorest neighborhoods in Willowsfield so Momma gives her all to provide the children with an alternative outside of running the streets 24/7 and getting into trouble. I come down whenever I can to help the kids with homework and to just be a big sisterly type figure with them. Really, most of these children need someone to talk and look up to that's worth something. If they had that, most of this attention-seeking b.s. wouldn't be going down.

Outside of a little drama, everything ran pretty cool. There are times when the children get into it, but we've never had a fight before in the four years of us doing this project - not even with the older teenagers that we provide service to either! Momma made it perfectly clear that she wasn't having all that.

We created a li'l' block party for the residents to hopefully attract more children to join up with us. We had several workshops dealing with a range of topics. We had culinary students from a few of the career tech colleges making food for everybody. They threw down too! D was working on one of the Carswell portable DJ booths, giving us our soundtrack of the day. Our efforts worked too as seventy people - sixty-five children and five adults - committed to coming over to participate and volunteer respectively.

Along with DJ'ing, D also hosted a five-on-five basketball tournament that attracted a lot of people. Guys from Pendleton Holmes tried to come down and beat the team of Blaze, Polo, Sean, 'Marcus, and Keith. It's safe to say that trying is all they did!

To be honest, a lot of people came down to the block party just to see D. For example, some of the older boys from the neighborhood started coming down to see if they could play him one-on-one for money. Mind you, he originally wasn't even playing in the game. He was too busy playing songs and working the mini DJ booth. But they were serious about seeing D in basketball, so he decided to give them what they wanted...

I just shook my head when I heard about it. I guess they haven't heard about D's basketball skills on the westside. D could be the best high school basketball player in the state! Polo and the other guys tried to give the boys from Pendleton Holmes a fair warning about how nice D is on the court, but they wouldn't listen. But D just let his game do the talking. When it was all said and done, the Pendleton Holmes boys lost about $300! That's what they get for being too cocky though! D straight took them to school!

Faith, Theresa, Dasia, Allison, and I stayed with Crystal, Victoria, Lyric, and the Sigma Beta girls. We went into the Pendleton Community Center and just talked with some of the girls about college life, boys, music, hair, haters, and career goals. It was really nice too. The Sigma's even taught us how to step! For all we did, my team deserved to get first place! Everybody had fun and even learned something.

♠♠♠♠

Polo & Lyric

I guess I must be Cupid or something now? Everybody keeps coming to me trying to get me to hook them up with people! I don't have a problem with it, but who officially made me the relationship expert? As everything was winding down in Pendleton Homes, Polo came up to me as I was talking to Faith and Theresa and said, "Aye, 'Liyah, let me talk at you for a second."

When he said that, I already knew what it was for. He wanted me to put him on a girl, I guessed it was one of the Sigma Beta's since Polo definitely isn't scared to talk to females older than him. But he really surprised me when he told me who he wanted me to hook him up with.

"What's up with Lyric?" he came out and said when we went to a private place to talk.

I smiled. "You wanna talk to Lyric?"

Polo cockily smiled. "Yeah, your cousin is fly! I was talking to her earlier and she seems like the type of female I need on the team."

I was still surprised that Polo wanted to get with Lyric! They'd really be perfect for each other. Both of them are known for their communication skills and getting what they want from anyone. If they started going out, that would be very interesting…

"I'll see what I can do."

"Cool! That's all I need for you to do."

After our conversation, I immediately went over to Lyric and told her about Polo wanting to talk to her. She was about as surprised as me!

"What? Polo really wants to talk to me? Stop lying, 'Liyah!" she said to me.

"I swear I'm telling the truth, Lyric! We just talked about it. So what's up?"

She shrugged her shoulders. "Polo is funny and cute, but I heard he's a player and I've had enough of those!"

"I know exactly how you feel Lyric, but come on! Do you think I'd intentionally steer you wrong?"

"I don't believe you would."

I continued, "Well, trust me on this one. Polo's not a player like you think. They just call him that because of all the girls that try to talk to him. But he knows how to act when in a relationship, assuming that's where it goes. He specifically told me to come and talk to you about him! That definitely tells you something."

She thought about it. "It wouldn't hurt to start back being exclusive with someone again. I haven't seriously talked to anybody since Cameron broke up with me."

I just shook my head when she brought up his name. Cameron is a guy that she was dating during 8th grade last year that she fell in love with. When he got his driver's license and moved up into 11th grade, he immediately broke up with Lyric and started messing around with different jump-offs around Willowsfield. Lyric wasn't trying to give Cameron the goodies and he decided to move on. Lyric was devastated. He was the one that got her. ☹

"This is exactly why Polo would be great for you. You already know I wouldn't hook you up with anybody that'll hurt you. You've been like a big sister to me my whole life. This is me paying you back for all you've done."

She smiled. "Aww! If you're that sure about Polo, I'll give him a chance."

A few minutes later, as we were riding back to the college campus, Lyric and Polo were in the back of the bus hitting it off pretty well. I'd never seen her as happy around a guy since Cameron. I smiled, feeling accomplished. I guess Cupid strikes again!

♠♠♠♠

Life Is Good

After the community service day festivities, HoodTalk 98.1 hosted a celebratory pep-rally/concert at Willowsfield University. It was nice too! The different Greek organizations stepped against each other, Miss Carter and Alana performed, and we won first place in the service competition! I immediately snagged the Hollister and Visa gift cards. They can have the rest of the prizes; that's all I wanted!

There were some hating people saying that the whole competition was rigged because we won and both D and I were on the team that got first place. Obviously they weren't getting the point of this event. We didn't wake up at four o' clock in the morning to see which prizes you can win for doing the most work. Yeah, that was an added incentive, but it wasn't necessary. We came to help out and serve the community. So all these selfish, hating, bitter people can chill with all the talk about the contest being rigged!

Other than that last part, the rest of my day went smoothly. Our trip to Pendleton Homes was fantastic and it was great to converse with so many like-minded, intelligent young women. Crystal gave me some great advice that I'm most definitely going to use as the election race rolls on. There are times when I feel like I'm taking this student body president thing too far, but then I recall who I'm running against and think again. I literally can't let Latasha win this election! How would that look?

Sincerely,

Aaliyah Anderson

♥♥♥♥♥♥♥♥♥♥♥♥♥♥♥♥♥♥♥♥♥♥♥

A Troubled Soul

September 23, 2012 7:32 a.m.

I swear, Jakiyah just continues to disappoint me! I'm starting to agree with D; I wonder why I hang around her myself. She's *nothing* but trouble and that is the complete truth. Jakiyah got jumped by those girls a month ago and she never got her chance to get a rematch. So ever since that crazy day, 'Kiyah has been literally trying to track them down!

That girl has been going to their houses knocking at the doors trying to get them to come out. She's been going to their churches waiting after service to fight them. 'Kiyah's even tried to go up to their jobs.

She is obsessed! I understand her being frustrated, but she's taken this to a whole different level.

I even told her that on the phone that day I got into it with Mariah and Roxanne came to our "father's" house to sign us to a contract for Carswell. She was telling me about how she was about to start searching all over the city to find them because she felt they were tryin' to hide from her.

I said, "'Kiyah, you're taking this way too far! Let it go! I know how it is in Riverstone Creek about losing a fight, but this hunt for a rematch has gone on completely too long. I believe it's time for you to just move on."

Good advice, right? Well, not to 'Kiyah…

"Naw, 'Liyah, forget that! I'ma find them and make sure they get what they deserve! I told you I got my squad up now! If they really wanna hit, we can do whatever."

I just shook my head and decided to move onto another subject. I hoped and prayed that she'd figure out on her own that this situation she was putting herself in was stupid. But, a month later, she's still tripping!

Last night, I had to bail 'Kiyah out of jail for trespassing and assault. From what I was told, she went over to one of the girl's houses for the second time and waited for someone to come out. Her mom was about to go to the grocery store when 'Kiyah attacked her like she was crazy. One of the girls she was looking for came to her mother's rescue, then they started fighting!

To make a long story short, the neighbors called the police on 'Kiyah and they came and arrested her. She'd been sitting in there since seven in the morning. No one, not even her mother, would put up the $200 to bail her out. So she called me…

Being the loyal friend that I am, I got Momma and we went down to the station to pay her bail off. I used $200 from the $350 dollars that I've been saving from my Carswell paycheck and all the other business ventures I have going on. I swear, no one can tell me that I'm not a good friend! Many people would've let 'Kiyah's stupid, naïve self stay in jail. She has to learn somehow. I honestly thought about it, but decided not to because that would be dirty!

As we were taking Jakiyah back down to her house in Riverstone Creek, she turned to me and said, "Thanks for havin' my back, 'Liyah. That really means a lot to me."

I ignored her. She's really been angering me with how she's been acting as of late. It's really uncalled for! 'Kiyah needed to be told about herself and, at that point in time, I was the perfect person to do so.

"So it's like that, huh?" she said after I didn't reply to her comment.

"Well, I guess it is! I told you to drop that whole thing with those Booker T girls but, like always, you didn't listen to me. If you had just moved on, none of this would've even happened. That was $200 of my hard-earned money that I used to bail you out!"

"Come on, 'Liyah! You already know I'ma pay you back."

"Oh, I know you are. But you're gonna do more than that! I've gotten tired of hearing about what drama 'Kiyah is in or who 'Kiyah is gonna argue with and fight against. We're a few months away from high school! That behavior has to stop." I sighed and continued, "I want you to promise me that you'll change your attitude. And I want you to mean it too. Put it on everything! It hurt me to see you behind that cell. It hurt even more to pay all that money to get you out! I still want my $200 back, but the best payment you can give me is you finally calming down. I want this to never happen again. I want us to both be walking down that aisle getting our high school diplomas in a couple of years."

She smiled and said, "Alright, 'Liyah. I understand what you're saying. I'ma chill out. Thanks for caring for me. If anybody, I know you're gonna be here for me."

I smiled and gave her a hug, hoping she really listened to what I had to say. My first weekend living with Momma full time was fantastic! Even though I had to, once again, get 'Kiyah out of something she stupidly put herself in, things still were great. Especially the community service day! We won first place and everything. Hey, speaking of that, let me go on and order me some more clothes from online with this Hollister gift card...

Sincerely,

Aaliyah Anderson

❤❤❤❤❤❤❤❤❤❤❤❤❤❤❤❤❤❤❤❤❤

Runaway

September 28, 2012 10:35 p.m.

I just got a really disturbing call from Allison's parents yesterday that I can't seem to get off of my mind. Since Monday, Allison hasn't been coming to school. I just assumed that she was sick, but her mom called and told me what was really going on.

"Long story short, we got into an argument about her attitude around the house and she ran off. We thought she may have walked down to talk with you."

"She hasn't come down here, Mrs. Pivot. If you want me to, I'll get my mom and we'll go look for her."

It sounded like she was about to break down and start crying in the background. Mr. Pivot took the phone and said, "That won't be necessary, Aaliyah, but thank you. If you hear anything from her, please call us. Have a good night."

"You too," I replied

I immediately started to worry. Allison has been going through a lot over the past few months, from that guy constantly harassing her to Wyatt trying to gangbang and pushing her to the ground when he fought those guys from Worthington a couple of weeks back. I could tell she was still taking Wyatt's change in behavior hard, even though she tried to hide it in school.

From what Allison told me a couple of days ago, she and Wyatt have been getting into it like crazy at the Pivot house, but she's the one that always gets argued with and blamed for "attacking her brother". Allison, who is usually calm and level-headed, has even started snapping back at her parents. I don't know how they couldn't tell that anything was wrong! Now Allie has run away.

At school the next day, I heard rumors that she was staying at Latasha's mom's house on the north side in Riverview. It really made me wonder why she wouldn't stay with me. It also made me mad that she'd go to Latasha for her problems instead of me. What's really going on?

I tried to call her when I was at Carswell that afternoon, but she wouldn't answer. I never blow up anybody's phone, but I called her three times after that. I still got no answer. The fact that she wouldn't answer any of my calls made me really suspicious. Allison always answers her phone, no matter who's calling.

Something is definitely going on that I need to get solved. What made Allison so mad that she'd want to run away? I mean, it seems as if she lives a perfect life. Allie has a mom and dad that love and care for each other, a super cool older sister, and a somewhat nice older brother. Plus, her family is sitting on a stack of money. What could be difficult for her? At least she has the luxury of being able to argue with Wyatt. If I tried to argue with Jeff, he'd probably knock me out with no hesitation!

Anyways, I hope and pray Allison is okay. I know I'm a li'l' distraught that she decided to go and find comfort in Latasha, but as long as she's safe, everything's cool.

Sincerely,

Aaliyah Anderson

♥♥♥♥♥♥♥♥♥♥♥♥♥♥♥♥♥♥♥♥♥♥♥

The Worst Possible Outcome

September 30, 2012, 12:21 a.m.

I know I shouldn't be writing at a time like this, but it's the only way I can keep myself from going crazy crying. We are currently at the hospital waiting for an update on Allison. She was brutally attacked by Gabriel and his friend Brandon. If we didn't find her when we did, I'm afraid something even worse would've happened.

Allison had been at Latasha's house the whole week. Yesterday, she was walking to the Northside Market and decided to finally call me back.

"Allison! Are you alright? What's going on?" I asked after I saw it was her number.

"I'm good, Aaliyah. I've just been at 'Tasha's house for a few days. It just isn't a good time to be at my parents' house right now, especially with Wyatt tripping like he is."

"So that's the problem? Wyatt's still acting crazy and everything?"

"Yes, and I've gotten completely tired of it! He's been trying to get down with the Rydahz and stay in the street, but I'm the one that gets fussed at and punished for trying to set him straight. They always stay that I 'start arguments with him'. Why is that? Why is it that no one listens to me when I try to tell them things?"

"Allison, Allison! Calm down! I'm listening to you right now."

I could tell she was crying. "I know, Aaliyah. It seems like you're the only one that actually cares about me."

"Well, why didn't you come down to the house and talk to me? You know the door is always open for you."

"I knew that my parents would assume that I was over with you. Your mom probably would've told them too. I just need a break."

"I totally understand, Allie. I just wanted to make sure you were okay. When you stopped coming to school, I was worried. Then your parents called me asking where you were. You have no idea how paranoid I've been over the past few days."

"I apologize for that because I really should've told you. But I honestly wasn't thinking straight. I just wanted to get away from them."

"Just remember what I said, Allie: you're never alone. If you have any problems, I'm always here."

"Thanks, Aaliyah. I gotta go. I love you."

I smiled. "I love you too, girl."

I just knew everything would be okay for Allison after I finally talked to her. I just knew it! I just knew after she saw that she had a friend that she could turn to for her problems she'd come back. I honestly don't know what I'd do without her.

That was the last conversation that I had with her before the incident with Gabriel. I swear, I feel responsible for her being in this hospital bed! I could've said something to convince her to at least come to my house. But I didn't, and Gabriel caught Allison at the most weakest and vulnerable point in her life by far.

Later on, Momma decided that she wanted to go down to the Northside Market to buy a few groceries. I went with her, hoping that Allison would still be at the store. *Maybe I can convince her to come back with us,* I thought. But she wasn't there. However, as we left the market, I found something that triggered my worst fears for Allison with her being out on these cold, evil Willowsfield streets alone.

Many people that live in Brentwood walk down to the Northside Market to save gas. It's located almost directly behind the neighbor-hood. Everybody uses the same way too. There's a li'l' alley in between Brunswick Drive that leads you directly to the Market. Momma and I were walking through that alley and I happened to find a dropped iPhone.

I curiously picked it up and saw that it was Allison's. The phone's screen was cracked, but usable. I immediately got worried and para-noid about what might have happened to her.

"Momma, this is Allison's phone."

"Really? Let me see it."

I gave it to her and she looked at it.

Momma then shook her head. "This is definitely Allison's phone, but that doesn't mean anything happened. Maybe she dropped it."

"Momma, Allison would never just drop her phone. She always keeps it sealed up tight in her handbag. She had to be about to use it."

Fortunately, I knew the password to her phone. After I unlocked it, an incomplete text message to Dante immediately came up. He had texted her five minutes after I called him to give an update on how she was doing. Obviously, by looking at his message, he tried to connect with her and something happened where she wasn't able to type the rest of the reply.

"See, Momma, look at what immediately popped up when I put the password in. Something is definitely up."

"'Lili, you could be right, but don't jump to conclusions too quickly. That's how unnecessary things happen. Do you hear me?"

I just nodded and continued our walk back to the house in silence. I now knew for a fact that something was going on and I needed to get to the bottom of it.

♠♠♠♠

The Search

When I got home, I decided that I needed to go find Allison. I needed to know that she was okay. Usually, I would've talked to D about how I was feeling and we probably would've gone out to look for her together, but he was on a football road trip. I didn't call him because I didn't want to get him off of his game. If I told him what I was about to do, I knew he'd be worried sick about me.

Even though D wasn't here, I knew I still needed to go and attempt to find out where she was. So I called for some back up. I definitely didn't need to be out in the streets alone by myself at night, so I called Jay and 'Kiyah. I know for a fact that if something crazy pops off I'll be good because I got two of the best fighters in Willowsfield with me.

And trust me, they were needed...

Jay was down at my house about five minutes after I called him. I told him everything about what happened and he said, "Well, if I knew we were going to ride on somebody, I would've brought my strap."

"Come on, Jay! You gotta think about it. We're black walking around on the north side at night. We don't need any extra problems so it's good you didn't bring your gun."

"I'm just saying, it would've made things easier."

I laughed for the first time in a while. "I think we're good, Jay."

About a minute later, 'Kiyah's mom dropped her off. I ran upstairs to get my flashlight. We then went out to search for Allison. We didn't even have to find her; I just wanted to know that I at least attempted to help. We pretty much walked around the whole area of North Willowsfield. From the mall back to the Northside Market, we searched and didn't find anything.

"Man, Liyah, it's been two hours and we haven't found anything! Can we just go back to your house and say we tried? Your mom's right, she probably just dropped her phone and didn't realize it,"

'Kiyah whined as we reached an abandoned road full of broken-down, vacant houses.

She was really angering me with how dismissive she was being about this whole situation. 'Kiyah had been complaining the whole time we were out. She made me regret that I even called her. Thinking back, maybe I should've called Dasia…Well, in the end, 'Kiyah was a big help but she was really annoying me during the time we were trying to find Allie.

I finally just snapped and said, "No! I'm not gonna rest until I know Allison is okay! If you have a problem with it, you can go on and leave."

'Kiyah snapped back, "What is it with you and this white girl? What has she done that's made you so loyal to her that you'll be out at eleven o'clock in Willowsfield trying to find her?"

"I guess you wouldn't understand anything about loyalty. Allison's been there at my strongest times and at my weakest times. That girl is one of the reasons why I haven't gone crazy! She's always so cool and she's keeps me level-headed too. I hate when people try to mess with her. She's my best friend!"

"So what am I to you, 'Liyah? Huh? Just some crazy broad you talk to? Because I know for a fact if I was in Allison's place, you wouldn't even think twice about coming to look for me! You even hooked her up with Dante when you knew that I've liked him for the longest time. What kind of friend are you?"

What 'Kiyah said had me heated. I angrily replied, "That's why you're mad at me? Because Allison and Dante go out? Are you serious? He came and told me to hook him up with Allison, not the other way around. Maybe if you acted more mature instead of trying to crack on people, argue, and fight every five minutes, Dante would've been interested in you!"

She started to get in my face. "I know you didn't just say that!"

I didn't back down either. I've gotten tired of being insulted and dissed all the time. I'm always doing something wrong in her eyes! Jakiyah probably would've beaten me, but I promise you, it would've been a fight!

Jay calmed us down though. "Can you two please shut up? Dang, man! I can't even hear myself think with you two shouting at each other."

I swear, when Jay said "shouting", I started hearing something coming from behind one of the abandoned houses. I said, "Hold up. Do you guys hear that?"

It sounded like somebody was screaming. I instinctively started running towards the noise. 'Kiyah and Jay came after me. I knew something was going on from the time we walked onto that street!

When we made it to the back of the house, we saw Gabriel wrestling with Allison, who looked pretty beaten up. He was trying to keep her still on the wall, but Allison kept fighting him the best she could. Her eyes were red. Her curly blond hair was messed up and her burgundy jacket was completely dirty and torn.

She kept screaming weakly, "Help, help! Somebody help me, please!"

When Jay saw that, he immediately went to work. He ran and knocked Gabriel off of Allie. He quickly fell to the ground while Jay got on top of him and started giving him non-stop punches.

Brandon tried to creep up on Jay with a sharp pocket knife. I shouted, "Jay, look out!

Jay, who heard me, managed to move away and gave Brandon a strong right hook that knocked him against the wobbly metal walls of the broken down house. Because of that, he dropped the pocket knife. Brandon somehow popped back up and threw a wide, sloppy left hook. Jay sidestepped it and hit him with a combination of right and left hooks that laid Brandon out immediately.

All of a sudden, Gabriel got the pocket knife and quickly lunged at me. I was so scared that I couldn't move! I just knew I was through!

But 'Kiyah pushed me out of the way and managed to trip him. Gabriel fell to the ground face first. When he stumbled back up, she ran up and punched him before he could react. Gabriel, who was already pretty messed up because of Jay, fell back on the ground. I then kicked him in the face out of frustration.

As we went to see about Allison, they ran off. We weren't even worried about them though. Allison was crying like crazy. She was on the ground and couldn't get up. Allison grabbed the right side of her body too.

"Oh God, it hurts!" she said through sobs and tears

Tears started running down my face as I saw Allison in so much pain. I immediately felt guilty. I know there's something I could've done to prevent this from happening. I just felt like I failed.

I had to erase those thoughts from my mind at that time though. We had to get Allie to the hospital! 'Kiyah surprisingly got down on the ground and hugged Allison. She propped herself up to the wall of the house.

"It's gonna be okay, Allison. We're here for you, girl," she said, looking up at me.

I took out the phone and immediately called for help. In five minutes, the whole entire block was surrounded with fire trucks, police cars, and ambulance vans. From the time they came and got her to when we made it to the hospital, I never left her side.

♠♠♠♠

An Update

2:45 a.m.

We sat up two hours waiting for a clear update on Allison's condition. 'Kiyah and I were the only ones in the room with her. Allie's parents left with the doctor. They couldn't stand to see her so beaten down. Wyatt was outside with Jay and Dante. They were planning to hunt down Gabriel and Brandon to finish what Jay started.

'Kiyah and I sat in silence as Allison lay unconscious on the bed. As I thought back to the argument we just had, I felt even guiltier. Was I really treating 'Kiyah that badly?

'Kiyah is my homegirl. I know if something pops off, she has my back. That's why she was the person I called to help me go and find Allison. If there's been distance between us, it definitely wasn't intentional.

"Listen, 'Kiyah, I just wanted to say that I apologize for what happened a few hours ago. I really shouldn't have snapped like that. You took time out of your Saturday to come and help me find Allison. If it wasn't for you, I'd probably be in a hospital bed too."

'Kiyah smiled at me. "Thanks, 'Liyah, but I should be the one apologizing. I really took it too far with all my complaining. I've just been feeling a li'l' bit jealous as of late."

I was surprised. "Really, why?"

She folded her arm and looked down at the floor. "It seems like you never have the time to chill with me anymore since you've moved to Brentwood. The first time I've really talked to you one-on-one is when you bailed me out of jail. You didn't even attempt to call me until Allison was in trouble."

"I'm sorry, 'Kiyah! I didn't realize that I was blowing you off like that. You know you're my girl and that's not changing anytime soon, no matter how many arguments we have."

She smiled at me and said, "You didn't lie about that!"

A few seconds later, a nurse came and got us to come back to the waiting room so the doctor could give us the new update on Allie. She had a minor cut across her left arm that could be easily stitched up. Allison showed no signs of being raped, but Gabriel and Brandon's attack left her with head trauma and severely bruised ribs.

I couldn't even hold back my tears. I walked out to the parking lot and cried my eyes out. I just know I could've done something to change everything that had happened tonight! A part of my spirit was broken seeing Allison lying in that hospital bed in so much pain. I couldn't stop the tears from falling. I just felt like disappearing into the cold night, never to come back again. Aaliyah messes up again - what a surprise!

I managed to compose myself so I could call Deangelo. When he answered the phone, the first thing he asked was, "Where are you and what happened?"

In between sobs, I told him what happened and where I was. Deangelo immediately said, "Don't move. I'll be there in a few minutes."

And exactly four minutes later, Deangelo hopped out of his seventeen-year-old sister's Camry and jogged over to me. I ran into his arms, feeling slightly better as I cried on his shoulder. As he held me and rubbed his hands through my hair, he told me, "Everything's gonna be alright, Aaliyah. None of this is your fault. You really helped Allison more than anything. If it wasn't for your persistence in trying to find her, she would've gotten hurt even more than she already is. Don't pile blame and regret onto yourself."

I looked up at him and smiled with red bloodshot eyes. "Thank you, Dean---"

He interrupted me and said, "You don't have to thank me, Aaliyah. Just know I'm here for you. If you ever need anything, I'm here."

I wanted to stay with Allison all night, but I had to leave because she could only have three people in her room at a time. The first thing I did when I got back to Momma's house was pray. I got on my knees and prayed that Allison would get through her pain quickly. I prayed that Gabriel would get his after the damage he did to her. I also prayed for myself. I prayed that I could get through this election without one of my sisters and guardian angels by my side.

Sincerely,

Aaliyah Anderson

♥♥♥♥♥♥♥♥♥♥♥♥♥♥♥♥♥♥♥♥♥♥♥

Aaliyah's Breakdown

October 9, 2012, 8:35 p.m. (Six Days until Election Day)

It's been rough going to school with the thoughts of Allison on that horrible Sunday night running through my mind. Nevertheless, I've had to push on. My grades have gone up tremendously because of the fact that I've dedicated myself to studying. The only places you'd find me at nowadays are at school, Carswell studios, and home. The only time I'm around anyone is in school and at the radio station. Karen, 'Kiyah, Theresa, and Faith come by to see me, but that's really the only interactions that I've had with anybody since the Gabriel situation.

I've been able to hide what I was feeling when I'm in school. To everybody else, I'm just the normal Aaliyah Anderson: Natasha Anderson's daughter, D's little sister, Faith's older sister. But I've felt distant from everybody else around me. It feels like I shouldn't even be here. *I should've been the one in that hospital bed...* That statement has gone through my head plenty of times. I just feel like I've done something wrong.

And boy, did it feel like that after the school news came on in third period!

Latasha was, once again, on the school news show this morning promoting her campaign. But today, she decided to take it personal with an all-out attack on me. It was totally unexpected and unnecessary! I haven't even said her name since I did the speech at the nomination party a few weeks back. She was just being dirty now.

"So, Latasha, there's only a few more days until election day at Clarkson. What would you say to anybody listening that's undecid-

ed about who to vote for?" the 11th grade girl serving as the inter-
viewer asked. They were recording live from Howard-Jones's high
tech media studios.

Latasha smiled into the camera and cockily said, "No one should be
undecided at this point. It's completely obvious that I'm the best
candidate in this whole campaign. I feel as if I'm the only one that
has been truthful and real between me and my opponent, who will
remain nameless. Why would you want to elect a president who
can't get along with teachers, keeps secrets, and can barely keep her
emotions in check? Really, it's your 8th grade year and you're just
finding out that you have a younger sister? I'm just convinced that
she was hiding Faith Johnson to hide the fact that her family isn't as
high and mighty as people think they are. And this also shows you
that my opponent isn't the perfect princess of Willowsfield that
people think she is.

"Then, look at how she's been acting around Clarkson as of late. Is
that how a representative of the students is supposed to act? My
opponent has been acting anti-social, depressed, and mean. Should
we have a president that can't keep her emotions in check? Yes, my
opponent did put on an entertaining and enjoyable speech at the
nomination party, but can she put all of her words into action? Before we go, I have a short video where we talk to a few teachers that
are totally against the fact that my opponent was asked to run."

The video played and all of the older teachers threw major shots at
me. While Latasha didn't say my name, most of these teachers
didn't even care enough to hide who they were talking about. I got
totally destroyed! I felt like a rapper who just got their career ended
with one song.

After watching that, every pent-up emotion that I'd been holding in
forced its way out. I ran out the library and to the girl's bathroom
and cried harder than I did that night in the parking lot. The li'l' bit

of makeup that I put on was completely ruined. I let off so many tears that my head started hurting.

"And this also shows you that my opponent isn't the perfect princess of Willowsfield that people think she is."

Her words just echoed through my head.

"Maybe she's right. I couldn't even prevent what happened to Allison when I had a perfect chance to. I've treated 'Kiyah horribly this whole entire campaign. I should've been there to stop her from continuing to go after those girls. I should've been the one in that hospital bed," I said to myself between sobs.

All of a sudden, the bell rang and I heard footsteps coming towards me. I didn't even bother to hide myself from whoever was coming.

Who even cares? Everybody probably feels the exact same way that Latasha does, I thought to myself as I sat on the floor, still crying my eyes out.

However, I saw that it was Dasia that was coming into the bathroom. She pulled me up by the arms and gave me a huge hug. "I just knew you were in here, 'Liyah. Don't let what Latasha said get you down. You're still the best candidate in this election."

"I told you I wasn't cut out for all this!" I said in between sobs. "I told both you and Miss Carter that!"

"Don't say that! You are perfect for this job. Latasha just used her resources to attack your self-esteem. She knew how you were feeling after that incident with Allison. It's time for us to use what you have."

I sniffled and wiped my eyes. "If you say so, Dasia."

She smiled and put her arm around my shoulder. "Trust me, I know so. You're gonna win this election. I know exactly what I personally need to do to help with the cause, too."

I managed to get myself together and I went through the day without any more breakdowns or negative thoughts. I still tried to keep to myself though. It seemed as if everyone was concerned about if I was okay after what Latasha said on the news. I was sitting in a booth at lunch waiting on Dasia to come over when dozens of people came over to me.

"Are you alright, 'Liyah?"

"Is everything okay?"

"Don't listen to 'Tasha! She was dirty for what she said. I'm still going to vote for you!"

I wondered if Dasia had told any other students about what happened with me in the bathroom. One thing's for sure, I didn't want anyone to think that Latasha's comments got to me. Even though they really did, other people don't need to know that! But still, I really appreciate everybody who was worried about me and cared enough to come over to comfort me.

When Faith and Theresa came over, I couldn't even look them straight in the eyes. I didn't want my li'l' sister to see me all messed up and down.

"Are you cool, big sis?" Faith asked me after they sat down in the booth.

I smiled and replied, "Yeah, I'm good."

"Everybody in my classes have been talking about what was said on the newscast," Theresa told me, "and everybody agrees that what Latasha did was lame and uncalled for too."

"And I especially don't like her using my name like that. I've got to talk to her. Somebody needs to set that crazy girl straight," Faith angrily said in her normal soft and calm voice. Even though I could tell that Faith was upset, she still maintained her calm attitude.

"That's not even necessary, Faith. We don't need you to lose your spot on the cheerleading team or anything like that because of some b.s. surrounding this campaign."

"I don't even care about that. Latasha doesn't control me. I have a problem with her dissing my sister and somebody needs to tell her about herself. Even though you're trying to act like you're not mad, I can tell you are."

I sighed. "Of course I'm mad, but I feel like we're taking this class president thing too seriously. There's no need for you to go and confront her. Trust me, she's gonna get what's coming to her soon. I don't know how or when but it'll happen."

I was completely right too!

♠♠♠♠

#TeamAaliyah Strikes Back

At the end of the day after the dismissal bell rang, 'Kiyah went up to Latasha at the bus rider's waiting area and straight up embarrassed her. She went off on her hard too! Latasha was scared out of her mind. 'Kiyah even made her run to her bus in fear that she would jump on her! I was at the car pool waiting area when it happened.

Dasia caught it on video and immediately sent it to my phone with a text message saying:

"This is just the beginning. #TeamAaliyah will win this election."

I shook my head and laughed as I wondered about what else she has planned.

Like usual, Roxanne came to pick me up from school so we could go down to Carswell studios. D was at football practice until 5:40 so I guessed I'd do my own thing until one of the other employees needed my help.

Key word *guessed*.

"So I guess you're not going to tell me about what happened in school?" Roxanne asked me after minutes of silence.

I was shocked. "How do you know about that? D must've told you?"

Roxanne smiled and shook her head. "No, D didn't tell me anything. One of your friends from the community service day got in contact with me and gave me a brief heads up."

I immediately thought about the text message she had just sent me and what she said in the bathroom.

"Latasha just used her resources to attack your self-esteem. She knew how you were feeling after that incident with Allison and Gabriel. It's time for us to use what you have."

I guess she counts being able to talk to accomplished and successful people as a resource.

After two more minutes of silence, Roxanne stopped the car at a red light and said, "You know you can talk to me about anything, right?" I nodded. She said, "Well, tell me what happened with you in school. I heard that girl you're running against in that student election took things too far with her comments and you felt horrible about it."

"Yup, Latasha straight up put dirt on my name today. I was shocked, hurt, and mad. I mean, how could she make this li'l' school election get so personal?"

"I totally understand what you're saying. I also heard that you took her comments pretty hard."

I sighed and lowered my head. "Yeah. I sort of broke down. This whole situation couldn't have happened at a more horrible time."

"Don't hang your head low, Aaliyah. I remember when *Hip Hop Today* first got picked up and syndicated around America, DJ was getting nominated for awards and everything while I was considered as his beautiful, but redundant, 'sidekick'. Then, something made me type my name in on Google and look at all the negative articles about me. I immediately went to my room and cried my eyes out. I just couldn't take it. DJ was getting all the praise and publicity while I got the public's hatred and scorn."

"Are you serious? What did you do after that?"

"Obviously, I didn't let what the haters say affect me. I worked to upgrade myself and improve at what I do and now I'm considered one of the best personalities in the media period. Man or woman, black, white, blue, green...whatever! I said all that to prove a point. Don't let what that girl said get to you. I understand you being down for a short second, but don't let that one moment sour your whole campaign and cost you a win."

I nodded and took in her words. When she was done talking to me, we made it to the Carswell Studios. Before we hopped out of the Mercedes, she said, "I hope you listened to what I had to say."

I smiled. "Trust me, Roxanne, I was listening."

"Somebody else is here to talk to you too. She can really give you some great advice on your current situation with this Latasha girl."

"Really! Who is it?"

Roxanne smiled. "That's for me to know and you to find out! Now let's go on in so we can get to this work."

It turns out that Alana, fresh off her huge concert tour for Carswell, wanted to talk to me and give some advice. Roxanne was right. Who better to tell you how to deal with haters than a musician? Everything she said was great, but there was one statement from her that just stuck with me,

"I look at people hating on what I do like this: no matter how much you dislike my music, at the end of the day, you're gonna still be at the same place you were yesterday while I continue to get better and more known. Come to think about it, haters are the reason why I'm here. I'm fifteen with a major recording contract! I just got off of a high-paying tour that attracted at least nine thousand people each night. The people that dissed me made me work harder to get where I am now. And where are they? Still broke and hating. It's just a sad, tragic situation!"

I laughed. She continued, "I know this is so played out, but let your haters be your motivation to step your game up. You just told me it's only six days until the students at Clarkson start voting. After what that girl said about you, what are you gonna do to make sure that you win?"

That was something to think about. What am I gonna do that'll help me bounce back after I pretty much got roasted, destroyed, and slaughtered by Latasha and the older teachers? I guess that's something I have to talk to Dasia about.

♠♠♠♠

Family Support

When D and I walked through the door of Momma's house after Roxanne dropped us off, I immediately saw Victoria, Lyric, Faith, and Crystal sitting in the living room with my Momma and talking.

"Come on in. We've been waiting for you, 'Lili," Momma said.

"Yup, 'Liyah, Faith told us about what happened with you in school today. Is everything cool?" Crystal asked.

I casually nodded. "Today was a rough day, but everything is cool now. A few unnecessary comments were said regarding me and my campaign by Latasha, but it's been handled. Everything's good."

"That's not what we heard. Dasia told us that you took her interview on the school news really hard," Victoria said.

Momma followed up, "And we all know that's not the reason why you were down. You haven't been acting the same since that morning after you came from the hospital. You can tell us what's wrong, baby."

I sighed as I walked over to the sofa and sat by Victoria, Crystal, and Lyric. D sat in the recliner on the side of the sofa. I guess everybody thought like Momma and wanted to know what's up.

"It's just everything that's been going on the past week or so. I just feel like I'm the reason that Allison's hurt like she is. If I had just told her to stay at the market, she wouldn't have been in that hospital bed. But I didn't and I've been feeling guilty ever since we found her being beaten up by those boys. What Latasha said was just enough to make me break down."

The room was in silence for a few seconds. Lyric was the first to speak up.

"Aaliyah, you shouldn't be guilty about what happened. If it wasn't for you, Allison could have possibly gotten hurt a whole lot worse."

Victoria added, "That is true, but Latasha shouldn't have been saying all that about her. It just makes me mad every time I think about it. I'ma---"

Momma cut her off. "We definitely don't need you anywhere around Latasha, Vicky, for her sake! Lyric is totally right; you shouldn't feel guilty at all. Now I need you to shape up and be the beautiful, energetic, and mature young woman we all know, love, and care about."

I smiled. "Thanks Momma. Thank you all for caring enough to listen to me."

"That's what family is for!" Crystal said.

An hour later, I was lying awake and working on a new drawing for me and Karen's comic strip, *The Misadventures of Ms. Independent*. At that time, I had just got off the phone with her. She was telling me about how she's finalized the character sketches we made. I can't wait until D gets around to making a storyline for it! We can start selling it and everything!

As I was about to close my eyes and start working on my picture, my phone started ringing. It was an unknown number. I was really slow to answer it. I asked myself, *Who'd be calling my phone from an unknown number at this time of the night?*

At the fourth ring, I reluctantly answered the phone.

Turns out it was Allison!

"What's up, 'Liyah? It feels like forever since we last talked."

"I know! How's everything going with you?"

"Great! I've been feeling a whole lot better. When they first discharged me, my head was hurting like crazy for a whole two days. It eventually went away though. I've just been chilling waiting for my ribs to get back to one hundred percent. It's actually been nice being back at home. Wyatt and I are cool again. He's really been helpful too! As you can see, I've got a new phone. It's a Samsung Galaxy S3!"

"What, girl? Why'd you turn on the iPhone like that?" I teasingly said. The iPhone actually was both of our first phones when they came out back in 2007. Since then, we've gotten every new model that's come out. Well, until now…

"This Galaxy is tight! It's a little bit bigger than the iPhone, but you can do so much. If I wanted to, I could talk to you for twenty-two straight hours without it hanging me up or anything!"

I laughed, happy to hear Allie's voice again. ☺

"That wouldn't be a bad idea if we had the time. It's been so rough not seeing you around, especially with this school election drama!"

"Don't even worry about all that! I'll be back at school in no time. Speaking of that, I just wanted to say thank you for doing what you did that Sunday night. You were my hero! I also heard about what happened in school today and I apologize. Latasha was way out of bounds for what she said. She took things way too far."

"It's straight, Allie. As long as I know you're okay, I don't care what Latasha or any of those fake, two-faced, hating females say."

"See, that's the Aaliyah I'm used to! You're gonna hold it down at Clarkson for me until I get back, Miss President?"

I smiled. "You already know, Allison!"

♠♠♠♠

Reassurance

The evening just continued its exciting surprises after I got off the phone with Allison. D ran up to my room and knocked on the door.

"Hey, Aaliyah, open up! There's somebody downstairs that wants to see you!"

I opened the door. "Really? Who is it?"

He smiled and replied, "You'll see. And trust me, it's gonna make you happy."

Wanting to know what was up, I quickly raced down the stairs in my pink Adidas tracksuit with a pink bandana wrapped around my head 2pac style and no make-up on. Honestly, I felt as if I wasn't looking all that hot. Of course, Deangelo had to be the one who was waiting to see me. Don't get it twisted; I was very happy and excited to see Deangelo downstairs looking as sexy as ever, waves spinning and everything! But I would've fixed up a whole lot more if I knew he was coming down.

When I made it down the stairs, I smiled and said, "Hey, Deangelo."

He smiled back and said, "What's up, beautiful?"

D chuckled. "I guess I'll leave you two alone." He gave Deangelo some dap. "It was nice seeing you again, man. But hey, even though I'm leaving you two alone, I'm still watching you."

We all laughed. I said, "Alright, D. See you later!"

D chuckled again as he walked into the kitchen.

I led Deangelo over to the living room where we sat on the sofa. After we sat down, I smiled and asked, "So what's up, Deangelo? What made you wanna come down here this late in the night?"

"I wanted to see you. I heard about what happened after you heard what Latasha said on the news and I decided that it probably wouldn't have been a good time to talk to you at that time."

"Did Dasia tell the whole school?"

He laughed. "Not exactly everybody, but Dasia has told a lot of people close to you."

"Well, like I've told thousands of people today, everything is cool now. I just got off the phone with Allison and she said she's feeling a whole lot better."

"That's great, but I'm more concerned with what's going on with you. You've been acting different ever since that day you called me to come down to the hospital. Yeah, Allison's doing better and that's fantastic, but I wanna know where your head is at right now."

I looked him in his eye and sighed. "It's been hard over this past couple of weeks. I really feel like I just can't control my emotions. Even now, I know I should be happy because Allison's ribs are getting better and she's getting closer to coming back to school every day, but I still feel guilty that she's even in this situation. Latasha was pretty much right this morning."

He nodded. "Your feelings are understandable. I know you've probably heard this a million times today, but let me say it again: what happened isn't your fault. You keep beating yourself up about it and it's not helping you in any way. I hate to see you in so much pain. I know you've tried your best to hide it, but I can see what you're going through." He grabbed my hand. "You're one of the most beautiful, intelligent, and strong-willed people that I've ever met in my life. You can't let this destroy you, Aaliyah. You have absolutely too much going for you to let Latasha or anybody make you second guess yourself. You hear me?"

I replied, "Yeah, I hear you," still staring at him. Deangelo was something special. His words hit me in a place that no one else's did -not even Momma's, Roxanne's, and Alana's.

I once again started to feel wrong and guilty. For the whole time me and Deangelo have been together, I've seemingly pushed him away. He's told me he loved me and I didn't tell him back. I haven't even allowed him to kiss me! Yet still, for all this time, Deangelo has still stuck around for me. He hasn't stopped giving up on me, even though I've given up on myself plenty of times.

"Deangelo, I gotta tell you something."

"What's up?"

I sighed and said, "I apologize if this relationship hasn't been what you've planned. I know I've been a horrible girlfriend! We haven't even kissed yet."

He smiled. "There's no reason to apologize. If you wanna take it slow, we can take it slow. I totally understand. We're too young to be *in* love anyway."

"Can I be real with you though?"

"Yeah."

I lay back on his chest. "The reason I've been trying to take things slow is because I don't wanna get hurt again. I've given my heart to other guys I've dated, only to get it broken. I really do love you, Deangelo. It's just that I don't want to feel the pain that I've felt with my past boyfriends again."

He wrapped his arms around me and kissed me on the forehead. "I keep telling you I'm not like the other guys you dated. Those guys are in the past. Let's worry about the future. If you swear you have love for me, you have to stop beating up on yourself for things you can't control. Can you promise me that?"

I smiled at him. "I promise, Deangelo." After talking to Deangelo, I felt so much better! It's nice to see that I have people that support me and expect me to succeed. I believe that I'm now ready for whatever will be thrown my way in the next few days leading up to election week. I'm ready for anything that's thrown at me period. I *will* win this election!

Sincerely,

Aaliyah Anderson

♥♥♥♥♥♥♥♥♥♥♥♥♥♥♥♥♥♥♥♥♥♥

The Damon Anderson Morning Show

October 11, 2012, 3:51 a.m. (Four Days until Election Day)

Dasia and I stayed up for hours on Thursday preparing for the presidential debate that was scheduled to happen on Friday afternoon. This would be my first and last chance to get at Latasha for what she said to me back on the news cast. Since that Tuesday when she put me on blast, she's gotten more support from a good amount of 8th grade females who admired her for "telling me about myself". Who knew so many people hate me? Whatever! All I know is that after how the debate went down, there's no way that she'll win.

Even though I said that I wanted to win the election without D's help, it quickly became obvious that I couldn't. After seeing me break down in the restroom a few days ago, Dasia immediately texted D about us coming onto the morning show at Howard-Jones. I didn't even fight the suggestion this time. I knew it was time to bring out the secret weapon.

D's morning show has grown very popular around Willowsfield over the past few weeks. His popularity for his show on HoodTalk 98.1 and as a correspondent on *DJ & Roxanne's Hip Hop Takeover* and *Hip Hop Today* really has put everybody on notice. Because of that fact, I was scared to go on the air!

Come to think about it, that's why I tried my best to avoid going to D for help. I could already have put a knife in Latasha's campaign, but I let my fear get the best of me. But I didn't have time to let it hold me down. It was now or never!

"You ready, 'Liyah?" Lyric asked me after the show went on a music break.

"Yeah, I'm ready for whatever," I said with a nervous smile.

Lyric laughed. "You have nothing to worry about, 'Liyah. We're all family! D, Vicky, and Polo host the show and I'm the executive producer. It's not like you're going to be doing the interview with people you don't know. Just imagine that we're all at Auntie Natasha's house on a Saturday morning just chilling talking about what's going on in school. That'll immediately take the nervousness away."

"Yeah, but what if I say something wrong?"

"As I said, Aaliyah, just imagine that we're all just sitting around talking on a Saturday morning. You wouldn't be worried about saying anything wrong then."

"Alright everybody, welcome back to the *Damon Anderson Morning Show*. This morning we have a very special guest in the studio: Clarkson student presidential candidate, award-winning artist, star tennis player, and my li'l' sister, Aaliyah Anderson!"

I smiled. "Good morning everybody!"

"Let's go on and get into it. For everybody listening at Clarkson and Howard-Jones, there's gonna be a huge series of debates going on this afternoon starting at twelve o'clock that will be recorded live from our lovely, newly-named Anderson-Smith TV Studios. However, the main matchup that everybody, from students to teachers, has been anticipating will go on at 2:30 between my sister and the other Clarkson student presidential candidate, Latasha Thomas. Now, on Tuesday's school news, Latasha made some very harsh comments about Aaliyah during her interview. If you didn't catch the interview, here is a small clip of it right here."

They played the part where she talked about Faith and said that I'm not "the perfect princess of Willowsfield people think I am". I lowered my head as I re-listened to her shots. Dasia, who was sitting right behind me on a sofa away from the equipment, came up and tapped me on my shoulder,

"Don't get down again, 'Liyah. In fact, get happy!" she whispered to me.

I was confused. "Why?"

She smiled. "You're about to see in a second."

When the clip stopped, D looked heated. I then immediately knew what Dasia was referring to.

"If you listen to the comments that Latasha made about the person who 'will remain nameless' and you go to Clarkson, ask yourself this: as voters, do you feel those comments were necessary? This is a school election, not the 2012 presidential race. Come to think about it, I doubt Mitt Romney and Barack Obama would start gossiping and airing out dirty laundry about each other. Let's be real here. Shouldn't a presidential election be about determining the problems and figuring out clear solutions? I wanna take a few calls about that after the next song, but I wanna get our guest's take on this. Aaliyah, what is your opinion on Latasha's comments?"

"Well, I believe that they were unnecessary. Like you said, D, this is a student election. Latasha's whole campaign is based on dodging important school-related issues to throw petty shots and talk about partying. What does our sister Faith and me not being 'the perfect princess of Willowsfield people think I am' have to do with the mistreatment that the students have been shown by the older teachers that Latasha represents?"

"You brought up a good point by saying that, Aaliyah. In the clip, she said, quote, 'I'm just convinced that she was hiding Faith Johnson to hide the fact that her family isn't as high and mighty as people think they are.' Why is she dissing and calling out the whole entire Anderson-Smith family? That's what I'm really mad about."

"Exactly! No one was trying to hide the fact that Faith is related to us. Isn't it a known fact? It's obvious that she's really reaching for something to say about me."

Vicky asked, "So Aaliyah, could you explain your idea for revamping the behavioral referral system? The current system has gotten a lot of criticism from both students and teachers alike. You've pretty much based your campaign around this issue."

"Yes, and the reason why is because something needs to be done about how the behavior at Clarkson is handled. Really, there needs to be a change in *every* school in Willowsfield's behavior system, but we have to start somewhere. I actually highlighted this in my speech at the nomination party. The reason why I'm so passionate about this issue is because earlier this school year I was randomly put out of the classroom by Mrs. Conner, who is also a Latasha supporter. Until then, I'd never been written up or sent out of the classroom in my *entire* school career. Mind you, I did nothing except ask for a pencil.

"Fortunately, I didn't get in trouble, but that situation brings up a major problem with the current write-up system. It gives teachers with no patience the ability to over-exaggerate write-up situations and get them in major trouble. I wasn't disturbing class. In fact, it was Mrs. Conner that really disturbed class. Minor and major class violations should be kept separate by some type of color code because, when dealing with school administrators, it's the teacher's word vs. your word."

Polo picked up, "What I really wanna know about is the other part of the plan you were talking about. I know for a fact there are some students at Clarkson who need to have an extra reason to stay out of trouble in class."

Lyric laughed and said, "You would know, wouldn't you?"

Everybody else in the studio laughed. Polo smiled. "You didn't lie about that! It would've been nice if we had a point system like Aaliyah was talking about in her speech back when we were at Clarkson. Maybe I would've stayed out of Principal Wittamore's office more."

D agreed. "Yeah, could you explain your idea of the referral point system?"

"The whole idea of the point system is to provide students with a reason to behave and stay in class. For some, it's not that easy. If I were to become president, the plan would go like this: for every day in the school week a student doesn't get written up or sent out, they receive a specific amount of points. At the end of the week, there will be some type of event that students with the required number of points will be able to go to. And trust me, it'll be worth the time being attentive in class."

Victoria said, "Aaliyah, it really does seem like you are very passionate about school issues and making a change. Are you planning to take the same energy into the debate this afternoon?"

I smiled. "Let's just say that I haven't forgotten those sly comments she made about me and Faith."

Polo and D said, "Ooooh!" I laughed and shook my head.

Victoria smiled at me and said, "Well, I guess there's your answer!"

D followed up, "Yes indeed! Clarkson and Howard-Jones students, make sure you check out my li'l' sister at the debate later on today at 2:30. Aaliyah's gonna chill with us for a few more minutes so we can take some calls. In the meantime, here's Frank Ocean's *Thinking About You* on WHJHS 90.5 FM. You're listening to *The Damon Anderson Morning Show*."

♠♠♠♠

The Debate

The interview on D's show went great! When I got back to Clarkson, dozens of people were coming up and telling me about how well I did and that they were gonna vote for me. Allison called me and showed some love too! Dasia was completely right. I was tripping by not going on D's morning show earlier in the campaign!

Ironically, Latasha listened to the show too and was "deeply apologetic" about her comments on the school news. But get this: she apologized to D instead of me!

"Yeah, she was talking to D about how she didn't mean to offend *him* by dissing your family," my homegirl Jazmine came up and told me a few minutes before the debates started. The whole 8th grade class got bussed over to Howard-Jones so they could see the debates live in the studio. Jazz is in all of Latasha's classes and was basically beside Latasha when she was talking to D.

I was immediately offended. "Are you serious? She apologized to D? If she should be saying sorry to anybody, it should be me!"

She shook her head. "I know, 'Liyah! She pretty much dissed you again. That girl knows she's dirty."

"I swear, Jazz, you don't understand how angry I am now!"

"Listen, don't even worry about it. You already know that 'Tasha be on some b.s. This shouldn't even be anything for you to get worked up over."

I nodded. "I understand what you're saying, Jazz. Thanks for the heads up."

Throughout the debates, every time I thought about the fact that she had the nerve to apologize to D instead of me for her li'l' comments on Tuesday, I got angrier and angrier. I was definitely ready to debate! What she did was extremely inconsiderate.

Then, to get me heated even more, Mrs. Conner and all the other older teachers that came down to Howard-Jones with us stayed mugging me. I really wanted to tell them off, but I held myself back. I didn't feel guilty about what I said on D's show. The statement I made about Mrs. Connor was true. If they have a problem with it, they can come and tell me about it!

On second thought, scratch that!

I'm not trying to get in trouble or anything like that. They are teachers, after all. They're just begging for a reason to put me on blast. I wasn't even worried about it though. All I was thinking about was my debate with Latasha. She definitely needed to be put in her place and I was the best person to do it!

I really feel like I owned the debate. I pretty much exposed Latasha's blatant disinterest in real school issues. From the alternative school situation and my plans for a new behavior system to the need for better classroom instruction, I was nailing her on every point. Basically, Latasha was standing up at that podium looking stupid and unprepared, especially with the very last question that the moderators asked us.

I have no explanation for why the girl didn't do better. The Howard-Jones students moderating the debate were the same ones that kept letting her come on the school news and talk about me. I would think they would've shown her the questions or something to make it seem like she actually cared about winning the election!

"This is a question for both of the presidential candidates. If you were to actually win the election, what are the first few things you'd do? Latasha, you can answer the question first."

It took her about five minutes to come up with an answer! In the end, she just promised more parties and fun events. Fortunately for her, a lot of the 8th graders could care less about school issues and they cheered for her. I just rolled my eyes.

It's gotten to the point where I could care less about this election. I feel as if I've put too much energy into nothing. I'm gonna end up losing anyway! In the end, all everybody wants is a good time. I've just started to accept it and the fact that it's highly possible that, after all my efforts, I'm gonna lose to Latasha.

I swear, I'm about to chill for the rest of this weekend! After all I've been through this past week, I feel as if I deserve it. I may walk down to Allison's house, but that's it. But, win or lose, all of this will be over on October 16th and I can't wait.

Sincerely,

Aaliyah Anderson

Forgetful Minds

October 16, 2012 9:00 p.m. (Election Day)

Even though I vowed to chill during the weekend and not think about the election, I just kept getting the feeling that I was forgetting to do something. As time wore on, I just couldn't figure it out for the life of me what it was. When I got to school, it finally came to me, but that wasn't what I was worried about this morning.

I literally woke up nervous! The idea that I could possibly lose this election to Latasha instantly hit me. If I was to lose, I don't know what I'd do. This goes way deeper than the election. That girl wouldn't let me live that down. Nobody would! People would probably still be talking about it in our senior year of high school.

"Latasha Smith beat Aaliyah Anderson, even when D was helping her."

That just doesn't even sound right!

After breakfast, Dasia came to the library. She seemed to not be nervous at all. Meanwhile, the thoughts of Latasha being announced as the student body president and the embarrassment it would cause kept running through my head.

"Today's the big day, 'Liyah! Are you good?"

I quickly replied, "No. I'm nervous like crazy!"

She smiled. "I knew you would be. It's sort of understandable. But I promise you, we will win this election."

"I hope we do. I swear, Dasia, it just feels like we're forgetting something."

Dasia shrugged her shoulders. "I don't think we are. I mean, we've done all we could do to gain support from everybody from radio, TV, and school magazine interviews to talking to teachers during their planning periods. You destroyed Latasha in that debate, even though it seemed like people didn't appreciate what you were arguing for. We've pretty much done everything that we could do."

Dasia was wrong!

I immediately thought back to the Willowsfield community service day when I was talking to Crystal about my problems with this election. She pretty much told me what I needed to do!

"Don't switch up your plans because those 8th graders aren't listening to what you have to offer. That's just one li'l part of the school population. Who you really need to get on your side is the underclassmen and the younger teachers."

Like Dasia said, we've talked to all the teachers that weren't supporting Latasha (basically all the teachers under forty). But none of us have even considered the 6th and 7th graders. Even though Crystal told me, I was still neglecting their vote! Dasia even gave me a heads up about it when she came to my house a few weeks back, but I marked it off. I was gonna change that though! And today was the perfect time to do so.

Miss Carter decided that it would be better if they went on and got the voting out of the way at the beginning of the day. Classes wouldn't officially start until every grade level and cluster got a chance to vote. I decided that it would be a great idea to talk to the 6th and 7th graders before they went to vote, if Miss Carter would let us.

And I knew that she would!

♠♠♠♠

Voter's Insurance

Fast forward to about twenty minutes later. The library was filled with students. All the seats were taken after all the 6th graders and two classes from 7-1 came in. As I looked around, I just couldn't believe that we both kept overlooking the underclassmen. Putting all of them in one room pretty much showcased that there were more of them individually than the 8th graders. When every class from 6th and 7th grade came in, Dasia and I counted to see how many students there were total. We came up with 415 in all.

I had to take a few deep breaths. It felt like my heart was about to beat out of my chest. 415 of Clarkson's 604 students were in that library and I had to convince them to vote for Dasia and me. I was extremely nervous! As cluster 7-2 started to file in, Faith and Theresa came up to me. I gave them each a huge hug.

"What are we down here for?" Faith asked.

"I just wanted to talk to you guys before you vote. Has anybody been talking about who they're gonna vote for?"

Theresa, who always has her ear in on what's going on in the school, got me up to date on what everybody was thinking about.

"To be honest, a lot of the 7th graders don't really care about the election. People feel like the whole entire thing is a li'l' show for the 8th graders that Miss Carter included us in to be fair. I'm not saying that I feel like that, but the 7th grade class as a whole feels neglected."

Faith followed up, "You know we're gonna vote for you no matter what, but you already know the cheerleaders are riding with Latasha strong. That's one major advantage she does have. Stacy and the other girls on the squad have been going around telling everybody to vote for Latasha and people are just agreeing to do it because they feel that it doesn't matter."

Theresa nodded. "Yup. You got a lot of fans and admirers in the 7th grade class but the pull Stacy and the cheerleaders have is strong, especially with the boys."

Stacy's another fake female that I can't stand! She's like a mini version of Latasha. Homegirl is next in line to be the captain of the Clarkson cheerleading team when our class moves on to high school. After she found that out, you couldn't tell her anything! She already has that li'l' light-skinned "I'm the ish" complex going on, just like her role model Latasha! Those girls are so arrogant and conceited! Because she's a year younger than us, I don't have many run in's with her, but I always catch her glaring me. I don't even react anymore. Females hating on me is like a natural occurrence now. I've just learned to accept it.

Hearing what Theresa and Faith said made me even more eager to speak to the 6th and 7th grade students. To assure that I didn't mess up, I made a quick outline of what I planned to say on a blank index card I found by one of the computers. I wanted to make sure everything was smooth and on point when I was up addressing the voters. ☺

Latasha can't win this election!

Miss Carter called for everybody to get quiet. It took a huge effort because of the large amount of people in that cramped room.

"Alright, everybody! Today is election day and in about an hour or so, everybody is going to start voting on who will be in the student council representatives of Clarkson Middle School this year. As I've said plenty of times, this is the real deal. The elected student officials will have a lot of power and responsibility and I want everybody in this library right now, including the teachers, to realize that. Choose who you vote for and support wisely.

"With that said, we have something nice planned for you right about now. Student presidential candidate Aaliyah Anderson has a few words for you before you cast off your votes. This was not planned at all. Aaliyah and Dasia came up to me about thirty minutes ago to ask me if they could do this. So, I'm gonna hand the floor over to them. Everybody pay attention!"

Dasia and I walked up to the front. I smiled and said, "What's up, everybody? Um, Dasia and I asked Miss Carter if we could talk to you before you vote for a reason. It's no secret that you guys really have felt left out when it comes to this whole election. I was talking to a few 7th graders that told me straight up that they felt like their issues and needs weren't being addressed. So, we're here to show you that we really care about what goes on in Clarkson with all the different classes and grade levels. So, if you have any questions, comments, or concerns, fire away. What do you guys really want for the next student president to do for you?"

After I asked that, the room got loud again. Miss Carter and the other teachers quieted them down.

"Alright, settle down, everybody! One at a time, one at a time. Voting doesn't start until about 9:30 and it's only 8:45 now. Aaliyah and Dasia can only answer and address all you have to say if you act like you have some sense," Miss Carter said.

Dasia pointed out one of the girls sitting at the table with Stacy up front. She pretty much tried to throw us off, bringing up Latasha wanting to have more parties.

"It seems like you're only concerned about academics and all that. I'm not sayin' that isn't important, but Latasha's been talking about how much fun we'll have if we vote for her. You haven't said anything about the fun things you plan to do. Isn't school more than staying in class 24/7?" she said with a li'l' bit of an attitude. Other students were starting to agree with her. The teachers just shook their heads and rolled their eyes.

The cheerleader girl then started giggling with Stacy and the rest of the girls sitting at that table. They thought they tripped me up. I looked over at Dasia, who motioned for me to calm down.

I took a deep breath and put on a smile. "That's a pretty good question. It does seem like I've left out a lot about the fun things I have planned if Dasia and I were to get elected to the student council. But I felt as if I didn't have to. I mean, come on! Think about it. I'm an executive intern for Carswell Media Inc. We have by far the best radio stations in the south, if not in America.

"I'm talking to all the 7th graders that were just 6th graders last year. Do you remember how Principal Wittamore had all these celebrities and important people in the community come and speak to us? Imagine how many music artist and celebrities we could get to come down to Clarkson. As a matter of fact, I can assure you that if you vote for us, we could get Alana Weber and Zayy Love to come down on the same day and do a concert for us. Also, it's gonna be one hundred percent free and everybody can get signed copies of their album. How's that for fun? Can Latasha do that for you?"

All the female students were going crazy after I said that. Zayy Love is an up-and-coming seventeen-year-old R&B artist that all the girls around Willowsfield love. A lot of people are saying he could be the next Chris Brown. The next *Chris Brown*! That's definitely special. His autograph could be worth millions of dollars in the future!

I knew for a fact that I swayed half of the room to our side and I wasn't even done!

"That fits into my new behavior plan that I'd present to the teachers if I get elected. Let me say this to all the guys: I'm not leaving you out either! I know a Zayy Love concert doesn't really move you but I know what will. How would you like it if the basketball players from Clarkson got a chance to go against D, Polo, and the future Howard-Jones Falcons freshman basketball team for bragging rights and school pride? If I was elected to be president, during homecoming week, we'd have different events where we go up against the students from Howard-Jones to prove we're the better school. And I know we can beat them too! Being a middle school doesn't mean anything!"

After Dasia and I were done, everybody - except for Stacy's li'l' cheerleading crew - was hyped about the election. Elijah even came up to me after our presentation was over and said, "Aye, that was nice, 'Liyah. You know you got my vote."

I grinned and gave him a huge hug. He made my day after saying that!

"Thanks, li'l' brother! Remember, I still want us to take a day where we just hang out and catch up on a few things."

He smiled and said, "I haven't forgotten about that. I'ma link up with you about it soon."

I wasn't just talking when I made all those promises to the underclassmen. I know for a fact that I'm the best candidate in the election because I can separate school business and fun. You definitely can't beat that! That's why I keep saying Latasha can't win. I put too much on the line to just lose out. Through these past two months, I've smiled, cried, and felt the pain of seeing one of my best friends in a compromising position. For all my hard work and dedication, I feel as if I deserve to represent Clarkson's 604 students as the president.

Well, Miss Carter said that she's gonna announce who wins on October 19th. That's one day before Howard-Jones and Jefferson face off. All I know is that, win or lose, I'm gonna be at the Howard-Jones/Jefferson game with Faith and my baby Deangelo (yes, I said my baby ☺). It'd be nice if I won though…

Sincerely,

Aaliyah Anderson

❤❤❤❤❤❤❤❤❤❤❤❤❤❤❤❤❤❤❤❤❤❤❤

Election Results

October 20, 2012 2:04 a.m.

Wow! Just…wow! What a day, what a day! I can't believe I actually pulled off winning the presidential election! I guess all of my hard work didn't go to waste after all. I was shocked when they announced me as the new Clarkson student body president today towards the end of fourth period. I had to double take because I thought I heard wrong!

I was out in the hallway when Miss Carter announced the winners of the student elections. She said that I won in a landslide, too. After the announcement, when I walked back through Mrs. Jones's classroom door, everybody went crazy! I swear, they had me feeling like I won a Grammy or something!

I feel relieved that this is all over and it ended in the way I had planned. I was really afraid that Latasha had gotten me after those disses she threw my way on the news. I thought I was done! But Dasia helped me work around it and we bounced back. I know for a fact that I definitely wouldn't have won without Dasia. I probably wouldn't have even had a chance! It really changed the whole game when she joined my campaign as the vice-presidential candidate.

I'm honored the other students decided to rally behind me at the last minute. This has to show all those old teachers that there's something special about me. Their girl Latasha wasn't even close to beating me! I wanna hear what Mrs. Conner has to say about that!

Everybody was coming up and congratulating Dasia and me on the win as we were walking to the car pool area at the end of the day. I was hugging people and shaking hands left and right. We actually managed to bump into Latasha, Stacy, and the cheerleading crew. Latasha was frustrated too! As I walked up to her and her cheerleading crew, she glared at me. They were posted up outside of the school library entrance.

I extended my hand. "Even though I won, I have to say that you made it interesting."

I kid you not, that girl looked at my hand, smacked her lips, and rolled her eyes. Look at me, trying to be the bigger person and show good sportsmanship. That's something they teach you in P.E. in elementary school. Well, I guess Latasha missed that class. Or maybe she wasn't paying attention. Too busy hating on me full time!

That girl had the nerve to say that I cheated! Is she serious? After she straight up dissed my handshake, she said, "Don't get too cocky! That election was rigged and you know it! How did you get a chance to talk to all the 6th and 7th graders an hour before they voted? That's straight up b.s.!"

I shrugged my shoulders, "Hey, I took advantage of an opportunity. Maybe if you weren't watching my every move waiting for me to mess up, you would've realized that the 6th and 7th graders are just as important as the 8th graders and teachers. Let's just be real: I was the most qualified candidate and *you* know it."

She laughed to herself. "Everything just always goes your way, huh? Perfect li'l' Aaliyah Anderson. Well, you better enjoy that student president spot while it lasts. You *may* not hold it much longer."

She got me heated on the spot!

"Is that a threat?"

She smiled. "Oh no, honey, that's a promise! You best watch your back."

She then pushed past me to make her way to the bus pickup area. Dasia held me back from getting back with her. I hadn't even been the president for ten minutes and Latasha was already scheming about bringing me down.

And I know for a fact she's not alone.

Winning this election has now put a huge target on my back. Mrs. Rockwell and Mrs. Jenkins will be keeping a sharp eye on me, waiting for me to lose my cool. Also, the cheerleaders are gonna be looking out for me too. And let's not forget all the girls who admired Latasha for "telling me about myself"! As if being Aaliyah Anderson wasn't enough, now the title of being "Mrs. President" is added.

Oh God, what did I just get myself involved in?

♠♠♠♠

Wyatt & Blaze

The announcement of me winning the election landed on a perfect day! Tonight is the night when Wyatt and the undefeated Jefferson Tigers face off against D and the undefeated Howard-Jones Falcons.

This was the last game of the season before the state playoffs start and both schools were going for the top seed. Wyatt has a lot to prove, seeing that Howard-Jones wasn't "good enough" for him! Like D always says, actions are louder than words. Yesterday evening at nine o'clock, the time for talking was officially over.

But they sure were talking a lot before that!

How about Wyatt and Blaze stopped by the Carswell studios yesterday afternoon at 5:45 before D's show started? It was a total surprise too! No one knew they would be there. It sure did shock me! Well, what Wyatt said to me really was the shocking thing.

"Yo, D! You ready to take that L tonight?" Wyatt said as he and Blaze walked into the HoodTalk 98.1 studios. They both were dressed in Jefferson Tigers navy blue and gold letterman jackets, gray 501 Levis, and navy blue Chucks with bright yellow shoelaces. I'm not even gonna lie, their outfits were definitely cute. But come on! Howard-Jones losing at home wasn't gonna happen.

D got up and gave both of them some dap.

"Wow, man! What brings you guys down here today?"

Blaze smiled and said, "You know, we were just in the neighborhood and wanted to see our man before he gives up his dream on an undefeated season."

Blaze followed up, looking around the studio booth. "Yeah, but don't even trip. You still gonna have your radio show and everything. You may feel ashamed to get on the air after the murder we're gonna perform on Howard-Jones, but hey, on Monday you can talk about our chances of going to the championship."

D laughed. "Okay, I see how y'all are tryin to play it! You think just because you shut out Hillman 48-0 last Friday you're gonna do the same thing to the 'Birds. I don't know about all that. I think you need to give up your dreams!"

Blaze smiled. "I guess we're gonna have to continue this li'l' argument on air. What's good, Aaliyah? We heard about you winning the presidential election at Clarkson. That's what's up!"

I got up and gave them both a hug. "Thanks, Blaze. What's been going on you guys? It seems like it's been forever since I've last seen you two!"

"Everything is everything, but aye, 'Liyah, I need to talk to you in private for a second," Wyatt replied.

I was sort of suspicious. After he said that, his whole attitude changed. He went from being happy, humorous, and excited to play against D to switching to the same dark attitude that he had that night at the hospital. He had to be about to tell me something about Allison.

We stepped out of the room and went into the hallway.

"What's going on, Wyatt. Is everything cool with Allison?"

"Yeah, Liyah, everything's going great with her."

"So what is it that you have to talk to me about?"

"I wanted to be the first to tell you this. Allison doesn't even know about what I'm about to say, and it definitely needs to stay that way. You got me?"

I nodded, hoping it wasn't anything crazy. But it sort of was…

He stuck his hands in his jacket pocket and lowered his head. "Homeboy Gabriel won't be messin' with y'all anymore. A few Rydahz and I handled that situation quick and easy."

My mouth dropped. "Don't tell me you guys---"

"Hey, remember what I told you. This has to stay under wraps. We don't want the police finding out all the particulars. If they discover anything, they're coming directly to you, Jay, and 'Kiyah for questioning. All they need to know is that Gabriel went into the woods to hide after you guys caught him attacking Allie and he disappeared after that. You haven't heard anything from him ever since."

I shook my head. "I can't believe you guys... I mean, do you feel guilty at all?"

Wyatt shrugged his shoulders like it was nothing to him. "Guilty for what? That fool kidnapped my sister. Then this man went to *Ghost Town*. We all know what he was planning to do down there! If you hadn't found her at the time you did, something worse could've happened. I don't feel guilty at all. We finished what you started and that's that. If you do somethin' crazy, expect to get dealt with. And that's real talk."

I just stood there in disbelief. I just couldn't believe that they would... I mean...wow! I guess you can never underestimate what anybody will do, especially when it comes to their loved ones.

♠♠♠♠

Jefferson vs. Howard-Jones

The game was going really well! It was everything I expected it to be: competitive, high-scoring, exciting, and back and forth. Every time D made a crazy catch, Blaze would go and give him one back. Sean and Wyatt were going at it too. Both of them were really performing well. At the end of the first quarter Howard-Jones was leading 7-14.

The atmosphere of the Jones Sports Complex was something similar to a college homecoming game. All the students were fired up, cheering for their respective schools. They even honored successful Howard-Jones alumni before the game. My joke of a "father" was one of the people they honored. The Howard-Jones and Jefferson bands and cheerleaders were going at it about as much as the football players.

You'd think you were watching scenes straight out of *Drumline* and *Stomp the Yard.* The cheerleaders were having a step off battle against each other. Victoria was getting down too! If Momma, Crystal, and Auntie 'Nessa saw her, they'd be proud.

Unlike the Worthington game, I just decided to go with Deangelo and Faith. He wanted to congratulate me for winning the election and I was down with that. ☺ We were having a great time together too!

I had to convince Faith to come with us tonight. This was her first game since she found out about our "father". I understand that she's still pretty upset, but that deadbeat isn't any reason to miss seeing one of the best games of the football season and the chance to support D. And she ended up having a great time with us in the end!

The Howard-Jones Falcons crowd died down when Jefferson got two straight touchdowns, both scored by Blaze. I guess all the hype was true; he really can play. Blaze is really fast, living up to his nickname perfectly. He's definitely not on D's level though! That's too far of a jump! At half time, the score was 21-17. Jefferson was putting on a good show.

My "father" was heated too. He needs to calm himself down! He was over there yelling at all the Howard-Jones players and trying to pick a fight with the officials. It would've been messed up if the police officers that escorted him off the field turned around and locked his crazy behind up. Are things that serious? There was no need for that huge temper tantrum anyway. Everybody knew that D would put Howard-Jones back in the game.

And he did more than that!

Howard-Jones was leading 27-31 going into the 4th quarter. I thought things were officially over. After seeing how Mario, Polo, and the Howard-Jones defense were shutting Wyatt and Blaze down, I thought we were gonna easily take the win home.

I thought wrong…

Wyatt decided to stop playing around and start ballin' out of nowhere! He threw a nice play action pass to Blaze for a quick touchdown. Jefferson was now leading with a minute and thirty to go!

Things were starting to get tense for Howard-Jones. Jefferson started playing that lockdown defense. The Falcon's lost the ball on a fourth down touchdown attempt. But fortunately for them, Wyatt threw an unnecessary long pass that was intercepted by Mario. There were seven seconds left.

I just knew D was gonna do something crazy to win the game. I even told Deangelo and Faith what I was thinking after Howard-Jones called their final timeout.

"D's gonna make a crazy catch and win the game."

Deangelo shrugged his shoulders. "I don't know about all that, 'Li-yah. Maybe their win streak is just gonna end tonight. They don't have that much time left to make a play and Jefferson defense is on lock down now."

"Come on, Deangelo! I have faith in D and I know he won't let anything get in the way of him winning this big rivalry game. Mark my words: D will win this game for us."

Faith nodded. "I hope so, because Howard-Jones really just got lucky. Wyatt throwing that interception wasn't expected. They have one last shot at bringing it home."

"That's why I say that D's going to win the game for Howard-Jones. In crunch time, he steps up!"

It turns out I was right too!

Howard Jones was on the fifty yard line and they made their best attempt to win the game. Sean, who was being trailed by three Jefferson defenders, threw it to D. And D did the unexpected, just like I said. He jumped over two Jefferson defenders to catch the ball with one hand in the end zone! Howard Jones won!

Blaze and Wyatt just stood on the sidelines in disbelief as the Falcons celebrated. They were so close to winning!

Deangelo and I went back to the locker room to catch up with D. A whole swarm of reporters had just left and he was in there alone.

"Good game, Mr. Superstar! That last play was crazy!" I said as we walked in.

He gave me a hug and Deangelo some dap. "I'm saying though, I have no idea how I even caught it, to be honest! And what were the odds that Wyatt would throw an interception? I'm still just shocked!"

"Well, Momma is gonna swing by and drop us off at Chili's. You wanna ride with us? Momma can drop you off at home like usual."

"Naw, I'm good. I'm gonna fall off in the after party and see what's happening. I know it's not my style, but we just won the most important game of the season. The Falcons are definitely headed to the regional championship! If there was any time to celebrate, it would be now!"

I smiled. "Alright, cool. Have fun and please don't get into any trouble."

He chuckled. "Funny, I was gonna say the same thing to you." I playfully rolled my eyes. He then asked, "Where's Faith?"

"Oh, she's outside with Victoria and the other Howard-Jones cheerleaders."

D grinned. "And where are you guys planning to go tonight?"

I smiled. "Why do you want to know?"

"Because I need to know. You said it yourself, things get crazy out in Willowsfield at night, especially after a football game. Remember what happened with Worthington a month or so ago? I wanna make sure you're safe at all times."

"Like I said, Momma's giving Deangelo and me a ride over to that Chili's that's in the Northside Mall Complex when the traffic dies down. Faith's going to chill with Vicky and Lyric. You know, nothing major."

He thought about it and nodded. He then gave Deangelo some dap. "Alright, Scoop. I'm trusting you to keep my li'l' sister safe. Don't let me down."

He nodded his head. "You already know I got you, D. Congratulations on the win again, man. It's a championship year, ain't it?"

D laughed. "You got that right."

It's so cool to see Deangelo and D connecting and vibing like how they are. It's important that the two most important guys in my life stay on the same page. ☺

♠♠♠♠

Confessions

Dinner at Chili's was great. Deangelo was the perfect gentleman. He paid for everything except the dessert, which I insisted that I pay for.

"It's okay, Deangelo. I got it."

"You sure, 'Liyah? I mean, today is your special day. I promised I'd treat you."

I smiled. "I'm sure. Just being able to go out with you is enough of a treat."

Deangelo smiled. "I swear, I don't deserve a girl as good as you. You're one in a million for real. Just like the song." I blushed. He continued on, "But one thing that I just can't wrap my mind around is how a true young woman like you would get with all these guys that treated you like a simple, teenage girl and not the beautiful, intelligent queen that you are. This isn't game. I'm speaking completely from my heart."

I sighed. "It's a long story that I---"

He finished what I was about to say, "Don't wanna get into right now. I totally understand. Just forget I said anything."

x

We boxed up our deserts and left. It was getting late, so we decided to go on to my house. We walked back to Brentwood in complete silence. I really didn't know what to say to him. I could tell he was a li'l' bit frustrated that I wouldn't tell him about Brandon and all the other players that I got with. Honestly, I didn't wanna tell him because I was afraid that he'd view me as the stereotypical, simple-minded, attracted to thugs and ballers, teenage girl instead of the beautiful queen he said I was.

After we made it to my house, I looked up into the dark night sky. The stars were beautiful! I always felt that I had some type of connection with the stars. Even when I was a baby, I always admired how they sparkled the sky in the darkness of night.

I broke the silence by saying, "The stars really look beautiful tonight."

All he could say was, "Yup."

I apologized in the most sincere tone possible. "Listen, Deangelo, I'm sorry for how the night ended. It's just that…it's hard to talk about my past with guys. I've just been hurt so many times. Please don't be mad at me!"

He turned to face me. "I'm not mad, Aaliyah. But answer me this: why won't you tell me, your boyfriend, about something that's been causing you a problem all this time? This is your third time telling me about how you've been hurt in your past relationships. Do you know how that makes me feel?"

"Do you really want me to tell you why I'm so slow to tell you about my dating past?"

"Why, 'Liyah?"

I sighed. "Because I don't want you to judge me because of all the mistakes that I've made. For my whole life, it's been hit or miss with the men in my life. And I feel like most of it is my fault."

"Well, let's talk about it then. Why do you feel that way? Why are you saying that it's been hit or miss with guys your whole life? Just tell me; I won't judge you."

We walked over to sit on the steps that led up to the front porch of the house.

"It seems as if I've always played second to everybody in my life. My 'father' barely has even looked at me since him and my mom got a divorce a few years back. But D sees him every day at practice. I'm not jealous of D in any way. I love him with all my heart. It's just that I feel as if I could've done something to grab my father's attention. That's why I originally started playing tennis. I just wanted to be known as 'Aaliyah Anderson' instead of 'D's younger sister'. It's alright sometimes to be called that, but dang!

"Then you have my two brothers: Elijah, a.k.a. Li'l Blue, and Jeffery, a.k.a. 808 Soulja. They're in the streets 24/7. Jeff's hated me forever. It pains me when he looks at me like I disgust him. It hurts even more when he doesn't look at me at all. I don't know what I did to him, but I wish I knew so I could go back and change it. Because of Jeff, Elijah and I aren't as close as we should be. If I was the big sister that I was supposed to be, maybe he wouldn't be caught up with the Rydahz. I neglected him from day one, something similar to how Jeff does me. He'd always try and get my attention, but I'd ignore him. He was my annoying li'l brother, my nemesis. I guess karma got me though.

"Then, I've been with and talked to about every player in Willowsfield. It's crazy! Before you, I couldn't even talk to a guy without them immediately…sexualizing me. Guys would always scheme on how to get their name popular in the streets by dating and/or taking the virginity of 'Damon Anderson's li'l' sister'. I was just seen as a simple way to get petty street fame. I guess my feelings didn't matter to them.

 "Other girls would look at all the guys I've gone with and couldn't imagine how I've stayed a virgin for so long. They weren't looking at my situation like it was good that I kept my innocence with all these guys trying to manipulate me for their own selfish gain. They said it like I should be ashamed, like I was a li'l' tease. It hurts!

Tears started rolling from my eyes. "Mistake after mistake! I try my best to hide in all this hurt so I can be what everybody expects me to be: Aaliyah Anderson; Natasha Anderson's daughter; D's li'l' sister; Victoria, Lyric, Crystal, and Jamarcus's younger cousin; and now, Faith's big sister. I'm trying my best to become Elijah's big sister again. Like Latasha said, 'the perfect princess of Willowsfield'. It's hard to always put on a show for everybody. I'm not a robot; I have emotions too.

"From day one, I've been hated on. Something was always wrong with me. If I keep my legs closed, I'm scary. If I was to keep them open, I'd be a slut and an embarrassment to the Anderson-Smith family. If I walk around like I own the city, I'm self-centered, conceited, stuck up, and arrogant. If I just try to be my normal self, I'm still self-centered, conceited, stuck up, and arrogant. I just can't win, can I?"

I looked in his eyes. "And I've never told anybody this. Not even D. I've held this hurt and pain in for the longest time. It feels so good to just…to just let it out you know? All I've had is my drawings. That was my only outlet. My way to let go of all the problems that were burdening me…"

After my rant, Deangelo leaned over and wiped my tears. After that he just looked at me. I wondered what he was thinking.

He then smiled. "I don't care what anybody says or thinks, 'Liyah. You're perfect. Like I said before, you're one in a million. I want you to realize that you're not alone. Not everybody is against you. You have people that love and support you. Please, stop holding all of this in. I want you to not worry about what anybody thinks. I want you to be the best Aaliyah Anderson that you can be. You don't have to live up to anybody else's expectation of you."

I used my arm to wipe the extra tears that were streaming down my face. I then smiled and said, "I love you, Deangelo."

He smiled and said, "I love you too, Aaliyah Anderson. Remember that."

I'm not even gonna lie, it felt great to get that load off of my chest! My talk with Deangelo ended a great day full of surprises and triumph. I can now go to bed peacefully, knowing that I'm not in this war alone and I have people that believe in me. ☺

Sincerely,

Aaliyah Anderson

♥♥♥♥♥♥♥♥♥♥♥♥♥♥♥♥♥♥♥♥♥♥♥♥

The Staff Meeting

November 1, 2012 9:13 p.m.

Before I start, let me say that I'm still grateful for winning the student presidential election. I'm still honored that everybody felt that I was the best candidate and would also successfully represent Clarkson.

But who knew being president would be this hard?

My first week in office was pure hell! If it's not one thing, it's another! What Bill Cosby said was totally true: *"I don't know the key to success, but the key to failure is trying to please everybody."*

How can I possibly please both the teachers and students at the same time? They both have different viewpoints on the school environment and different needs.

For example, I finally pitched my new behavior plan to the teachers on Monday afternoon so it could be officially approved. I worked long and hard the day before on a PowerPoint and handouts detailing what it's all about. I even made a petition and had Faith and Theresa go around the school help me get over 400 student signatures. Yup, I thought I was overachieving and representing the student body well.

Until the staff meeting…

I won't say that having to present my plan to the teachers and administrators was the major problem. To be honest, it was easy. But, convincing the teachers to support me was the hard part. Mrs. Conner and the older teachers picked my plan apart piece by piece!

"Why are you so sure that your method will work? I believe no matter what you try, students will still act like a fool in class. In my thirty years of teaching, the only thing that I saw that worked was when we used to have the right to paddle the kids. Now that's gone and we have no power in this new school system. We barely can discipline students without being reprimanded," Mrs. Connor said immediately after my presentation was over. Other teachers, both young and old, were starting to agree too.

I immediately replied with what I thought was a well-thought-out, intelligent answer. "Mrs. Conner, it's obvious that the landscape and structure of the school system and its students has changed drastically over the past twenty or so years. We now live in a 'what you can do for me' type society. My behavior plan, as I've said countless times before, will give the students an extra added incentive to perform well in class and act like productive young men and young women."

I swear, I felt like I was Oprah or Momma on her TV show. I broke it straight down, impressing the younger teachers and Miss Carter. Of course, the older teachers had to back me in a corner and make me look like I didn't know what I was talking about.

"All of that is well and good, but you didn't answer the question," Mrs. Jenkins quickly replied. "Why are you so sure that giving these children an incentive to stay in class would work? What's your reasoning for making the conclusion that all the students, even the ones that didn't vote for you, would just blindly follow your proposed guidelines?"

"First of all, eighty percent of the school voted for me so I really don't see anyone having a problem with my idea or following it blindly. Secondly, this is a new generation of students and certain things need to be change to fit how complex we are now. With all due respect, the old paddling method of discipline is long outdated.

Sending students out the classroom 24/7 isn't really working out either."

Mrs. Connor smacked her lips. "Well, if the disciplinary methods of old don't work, show me the statistics proving that. As a matter of fact, show me the statistics that say your ideas are as effective as you say they are. You can't be all talk and no bite."

That lady was really starting to anger me!

"If you want to see how ineffective the current methods of discipline are, just look at the percentage of office referrals sent to the office on a month by month basis dating back to last school year. If you wanna see how unsuccessful sending a child out of the class without them getting as much as a highlight of what was taught when they were out, look at the test scores and school GPA's for the county, Mrs. Connor. A minor class disruption shouldn't warrant anyone missing precious learning time."

"But you still haven't answered my question! What makes you think that this 'favor for a favor' style behavioral system will prove to be effective? Where's your proof? What statistics are backing you up?"

I let out a huge sigh and folded my arms. They finally shut me down! I had no stats to back up my idea and they knew it. They were having fun playing with me.

Mrs. Connor smiled and said, "See, how are we going to sign off on a plan that isn't even proven to work? This is a complete waste of time. Now, I have papers to grade so can we go on and speed this up?"

Miss Carter stepped in to defend me. "Mrs. Connor, you are way out of line."

"How am I out of line? Isn't this is what we all have been thinking for the past twenty minutes?"

Miss Jones, who usually is silent and non-confrontational, spoke up for me too. "I believe that Aaliyah's idea is great and should really be taken seriously. Something really does need to change around here. And mind you, this is the young lady that all the other students elected to represent them. That means they trust that she'll voice the concerns, issues, and problems of the student body effectively."

Miss Carter agreed. "Exactly, and we owe the new student body president the benefit of coming into our staff meetings and brilliantly pitching a new idea for the betterment of the school without getting destroyed for it."

Mrs. Connor rolled her eyes and leaned back in her chair. She knew her "fun" was over!

Miss Carter continued, "Now, I see both sides of the argument here. It is true that this is an unproven behavior plan, but it sounds good enough to work. Besides, the presentation was flawless. You really did your homework. I also like that you were proactive and circulated a petition around to the student body. I believe we should give President Anderson a one week trial to run the system her way without any interruptions. If things go well this week, we can consider incorporating her methods into our behavioral system."

She then turned to me, "So Aaliyah, that means you have a lot to prove and show for in the next few days. On paper this idea looks great but actions speak louder than words. We want at least a slight change in the school's overall behavior. We all are counting on you, Aaliyah. Don't let us down."

I smiled and said, "Yes ma'am. Thank you all for your time."

Presidential Duties

I thought convincing all the students to chill out with all the craziness would be easy. I mean, all I had to do was go on D's morning show the next day and talk about the Clarkson/Howard-Jones pep rally on Friday and all the surprises we had planned. The rest would work itself out, right?

I was completely wrong!

The interview on D's show once again went very well. We were all wildin' out and having a good time. I even gave a sneak peek of what was in store for Friday.

"Alright, everybody, welcome back to *The Damon Anderson Morning Show*. We have in studio right now Clarkson's newly-elected student body president, Aaliyah Anderson. It's actually very ironic that we have Aaliyah in here this morning because I want to address some rumors that have been going around the hallways of Clarkson and Howard-Jones alike."

I smiled. "What's going on, D? What rumors are you talking about?"

"In your behavior plan, you talked about having special events every Friday for students who stay out of trouble during the week and the first official event is this coming Friday. There have been rumors going around about what you, the Clarkson and Howard-Jones student council, along with the school administrators, have in store and I feel like it's totally unnecessary! I heard that you guys wanna put on an 8th grade vs. 9th grade, Howard-Jones vs. Clarkson All-Star basketball game to conclude homecoming week. Is that true?"

I laughed. "Yup, it's totally true and I believe that Clarkson will win that game and bring home bragging rights and the huge trophy that is planned to be given to the winning school."

"Come on, Aaliyah! That's just foolish pride! You know for a fact that Clarkson is gonna get slaughtered. This is high school! You kids need to go on back to the playground you came from."

Everybody in the studio playfully said, "Ooh!"

I chuckled. "So what are you *really* trying to say, D? That we have no shot?"

D shrugged his shoulders. "Exactly."

Everybody in the studio was tripping out! I replied, "Clarkson definitely has a shot at winning the game. There are several reasons why we have a chance, but I can tell you one major game changer."

D laughed. "This is gonna be good! What's the game changer?"

I smiled. "I'm playing in the game."

Polo laughed and said, "Well, we know for a fact Clarkson is gonna lose now!"

D started laughing again too. "I'm saying, Polo! Like, what kind of announcement is that? Aaliyah, we all know that you're a legend in Willowsfield when it comes to tennis, but don't go too far. Basketball is my game. You saw what went down in Pendleton Homes during the community service day when those boys challenged me. I believe that you're stepping in the wrong territory!"

"I'm not saying anything else until Friday. I'ma let my game do the talking!"

"It's gonna be pretty quiet out there on the court then!" Polo replied. We all laughed again. He's such a fool!

"Students of Howard-Jones High School, please forgive and disregard my sister. She obviously doesn't realize what's in store for Clarkson Middle School on Friday. As a matter of fact, call in and tell her how you really feel! Who do you think is going to take home the Homecoming trophy on Friday: Howard-Jones or Clarkson?

"Congratulations to Aaliyah for winning Clarkson's presidential race, but you're out of your mind for saying that the HJ Falcons basketball dream team is gonna lose to some middle-schoolers. Get outta here, man! Isn't it about time for *Dora the Explorer* to come on or something? Here's Rihanna & Future, *Loveeeeee Song* on *The Damon Anderson Morning Show*!"

♠♠♠♠

Saving Someone's Life

Not even an hour after my interview on D's show, two fights popped off. One of the fights was going on when I was walking to Mrs. Jenkins's first period class after I got back to Clarkson! It was two girls fighting over some boy. I just shook my head. Strike one!

Then, I was walking from lunch with Deangelo and Faith later on in the day and I saw like twenty Rydahz making their way towards the boy's restroom. That wasn't just a coincidence. I knew there was about to be some type of crazy gang fight. Tay, who was following behind the huge group of Rydahz, even confirmed it.

"Tay, what's going on?"

"It's nothin', 'Liyah. Ol' boy Jeremiah gotta catch this one because he violated the set by wearing Killas colors. Dude just straight stupid! But aye, they got it though. I'm just goin' to watch."

I just shook my head. It's always something!

If it was any normal day, I would've just walked away and let all those boys get suspended. It's not my problem, right?

Not today!

They could've possibly killed that boy in there. Then it would've be on me. Miss Carter and the administrators would go to the cameras and see that I possibly could've prevented them from fighting, with me being the student body president and everything.

"So Tay, how are things going with Karen?"

He cockily smiled. "You know, everything's good. She's really a fly female. We're just tryin' to take things slow right now, but we pretty close to makin' things official."

I nodded. "Yup, that's good. You know you owe me, right?"

"Yeah, I was aware of that. You need some money? You know I got you."

"No, I really need you to help me prevent all this craziness from going on this week. For example: I need you to somehow convince them to chill out with jumping Jeremiah. Please do it for me! If y'all get caught, I'll wind up getting in the most trouble because I'm the president."

Tay understood where I was coming from. "I can't call them off because I didn't set all this up and my rank isn't high enough. But I can get Dwayne so you can talk to him. Is that cool?"

I smiled. "That'll work, Tay. Thank you."

I knew it would be easy to convince Dwayne to chill out with jumpin' Jeremiah. He's wanted to get with me for the longest time, but I'm not even checking for him. He's cute, but I'm definitely not trying to date a sixteen-year-old 8th grader. He's older than D and he's still in middle school! Are you serious? Momma would probably have a heart attack if I brought him home!

But I've never straight up dissed him. We've remained cool with each other. So I just told him about how the teachers are all on my back about me trying to change the behavior of the school and how two fights had already popped off. Surprisingly, he listened to me.

"Aye, I got you, thug. We ain't tryin' to get you in trouble or nothin' like that. We'll just catch him back in Riverstone Creek."

"That'll work. Thanks for working with me on this, Dwayne," I said as I gave him a hug. He went into the restroom and like five seconds later, all the Rydahz started coming out. I let out a huge sigh, happy that everything worked out.

Now, I know it's messed up that Jeremiah is still gonna get jumped! I couldn't control that. That was out of my hands! But I gave him a better chance to run or do whatever he needs to do. If they got him in that bathroom, it would've been over for both of us.

Hey, come to think about it, I saved somebody's life today!

♠♠♠♠

Intentional Sabotage

Even though I prevented one huge fight, I couldn't get around to stopping the other face-offs that were suddenly starting to pop off between the 8th graders. Towards the end of the day during fourth period, I was running an errand for Miss Jones and I literally walked into a fight. There were three girls jumping another girl in Mrs. Connor's class. The crazy thing was that Mrs. Connor was just standing idly at her board like nothing was happening.

I immediately ran in and pulled the girl they were jumping away from them. Fortunately, two campus police officers came and calmed the other girls down. The officers then escorted the girls to the office.

I looked at Mrs. Connor like she was stupid. She looked at me like I was crazy!

"Mrs. Connor, what happened? Why didn't you prevent them from fighting? Why didn't you call the office sooner?" I asked her.

She laughed at me. "Listen, little girl, I don't have to answer to you! Nothing in your 'behavior plan' said anything about what to do when there's a fight. What, do I take a point away from them? What color office referral sheet do I use? I guess those four girls won't be able to make it to the game on Friday."

She had me so angry! Everything that happened today was just a joke to her. We've had six fights in one day and this woman wants to throw shade on my behavioral plan? I didn't even say anything else to her. I just went to the office and talked to Miss Carter about how I was feeling.

"This is ridiculous, Miss Carter! Six fights in one day! This isn't a coincidence. I don't know what, but something isn't right."

As I talked to her, Miss Carter nodded her head and put her right hand on her chin like she was in deep thought. Then she gave me some shocking information. "You're totally right, Aaliyah. As a matter of fact, I've noticed a trend going on with the fights that happened today. All of them happened in classrooms or in the presence of teachers that were against your new behavior plan."

My jaw dropped. "Are you serious?"

"I wouldn't lie about this, baby girl. To put even more proof on the table, none of those teachers even called the office for back-up when the fights were going on. It really does seem like the older teachers are trying to intentionally sabotage your plan."

I was shocked! Those teachers hate my ideas that much? Wow! All I was trying to do was convince the students to calm all that crazy behavior down. Is that so wrong?

"Don't even get down about all this, Aaliyah. We are definitely gonna get to the bottom of this. What they did today was uncalled for and I'm not gonna stand for it! We can't have students acting crazy and teachers allowing it because of a foolish disagreement of opinions! As a matter of fact, I want you to address the students during the afternoon announcements in a few minutes. Convince them to get their acts together like you convinced them to vote for you."

That wasn't a bad idea and I needed to make sure no other incidents popped off this week. So I channeled my inner Natasha Anderson/Roxanne Steele and talked to all the Clarkson students about why they really need to chill.

"What's up, everybody? This is your president Aaliyah Anderson with a special announcement. First off, I want to thank everybody that voted and supported me during the student council election. It put me in the position to say what I'm about to say now. We need to stop all the fighting! Altogether, there have been six fights this week and it's just Tuesday.

"If you didn't hear my interview on *The Damon Anderson Morning Show,* let me say now that we have a lot planned for everybody on Friday if things go correctly. That means that we as Clarkson students need to stop with all this unnecessary behavior. You voted for me because you knew you could rely on me to deliver all that I promised. Now that I've set up a huge day Friday, I'm relying on you to shape up your behavior and be front and center on Friday when we fight for school pride against Howard-Jones. I'll see you then!"

♠♠♠♠

The Woman Who Really Runs Things

After my announcement to the students of Clarkson, Miss Carter and I met with the teachers that sat back and allowed the students to fight each other.

"Alright, let's go on and get this out the way because I have things to do and Aaliyah needs to make it down to Carswell studios by four o'clock," Miss Carter said as the six teachers took a seat at the round table in the teacher's lounge. "Why is it that there was six fights and fourteen students suspended today?"

Mrs. Connor, Mrs. Jenkins, and the four other older teachers were completely silent.

Miss Carter laughed. "You know, it's funny that you want to comment and voice your opinions on everything but what pertains to you. Why is it that miraculously after Aaliyah pitches her new behavioral system idea and we decide to put her on a week trial run, there's a sudden surge of fights that could've easily been prevented? Then, to make things even worse, none of you teachers called the office to request that campus police be deployed for back-up or filled out a write-up form. Why is that? I want answers and I want them now!"

Mrs. Connor smacked her lips. "While you're snapping at us, you should be talking to your president about her dysfunctional behavioral system. There was nothing in there pertaining to dealing with students fighting. That's why---"

Miss Carter cut her off. "Don't even try and pull that card, Mrs. Connor. You know for a fact county and state protocol says that when a fight happens, you are to try and break it up or immediately get in contact with a school administrator or security personnel." She took a breath and continued on. "Now, because of all your negligence, we have to explain to the board of education why fourteen of our students are going to be suspended and unable to take their standardized tests on time. Then, that information is gonna leak to the media. If we're lucky, we may be able to dodge getting an article on WillowsfieldToday.com. They'll definitely have a field day with this situation! After that, we have to deal with angry parents who'll start to question the integrity and safety of this school. And this is all because you have a problem with a *proposal* for a revamp in the school behavioral system? Are you kidding me?"

Miss Carter took another breath. "You know I'm going to have to write each one of you up, right? This is completely unacceptable!"

Mrs. Jenkins looked like she was almost in tears when she redundantly asked. "You're really about to write us up for this?"

"Does it look like I'm playing? All of you have officially been put on notice. This is my school and you march to my beat or you can pack your things and walk! And that goes for any teacher or other employee of Clarkson Middle School that has a problem with how I run things." Miss Carter got up and slid her chair back under the table. "I'm done. Let's go, Aaliyah."

I was completely shocked! Miss Carter straight up told Mrs. Connor and the Teacher Mafia about themselves. You have no idea how satisfied I was! Coincidentally, after that meeting and my afternoon announcement, we didn't have to deal with anymore drama that whole week.

Word was getting around that the older teachers were bad-mouthing both me and Miss Carter to the students in their respective class later on in the week. Somebody even caught Mrs. Connor doing it on camera and sent it to my phone! She was calling us all types of controlling, two-faced, and fake. I immediately showed it to Miss Carter.

She just shrugged her shoulders. "Hey, as long as she's not saying any of that to my face, I'm cool. That's all they do anyways. They talk and gossip behind people's backs then try their best to dictate how things are run in this school. That's definitely not how things work! I like to keep it professional so I just keep what they're saying exactly where it's supposed to be - behind me."

I felt the same way as Miss Carter. If she's not mad about what they're saying, I'm not going to worry about it. Besides, we won in the end anyway!

♠♠♠♠

Practice Makes Perfect

Later on Tuesday night after we wrapped up D's show at Carswell, I went down to the fitness center with Allison to practice on the basketball court. It was my first time going to the fitness center in months! I've been so tied down with everything I've been doing that

I haven't even got a chance to work out on a regular basis. And I felt the result of not working out hard too!

As D said on his morning show at Howard-Jones, basketball isn't traditionally my sport, but I've always had a love for it. I guess it's all the games that I used to watch with D when I was younger. D's loved sports seemingly from the time he came out the womb! The only thing that actually kept me from playing is the fact that it didn't seem womanly in the slightest.

Back when I was younger, I couldn't tell the WNBA apart from the NBA. Those women had muscles, Allen Iverson braids, mustaches, and goatees! It seems like you have more feminine players in the league now. Candice Parker, Jennifer Lacey, and Cappie Poindexter are a few ballers that still keep things sexy.

Now I wanna start playing basketball. That's the reason why I inserted myself into the game. I think if I get my skills right, I could be a solid point guard. I swear, that position was made for me! A point guard is like the sports equivalent of a CEO on the court. They control the flow of the game. I could be a mix between Chris Paul, Ray Allen, and Tika Shumpter. Flashy, smooth, and sexy!

But I definitely needed to work on a few things!

When Allison and I first started playing, I was throwing up air balls and missing layups left and right. On Friday, my game was right but I had to practice like D. Allison and I woke up playing basketball and we went to sleep playing basketball. It paid off in the end too…

But I'm giving away too much!

Allison made my day when she said she'd officially be back at school by Thursday and that she'd be playing on Team Clarkson Friday at the homecoming basketball game on Friday.

"Really! Are you sure you're back at full strength? Things are gonna get pretty competitive."

Trust me, 'Liyah, I'll be good to go by Friday. I've been resting for weeks! I've barely been out the house. My body has gotten more than enough rest."

I immediately got excited!

"Girl, we're gonna be like the female version of LeBron and Dwayne Wade."

She laughed. "Okay, I have a slight problem with that comparison. Who's gonna be LeBron and who's gonna be Dwayne?"

I smiled and shrugged my shoulders. "It doesn't even matter. As long as we win like the Heat, we're gonna be good."

♠♠♠♠

A Brotherly Heads Up

Things were absolutely crazy on Friday! My day started super early as I got up with D at 3:30 in the morning so "we" could practice for the game at the fitness center. D gave me a few pointers and we even played a quick one-on-one game. Like expected, he murdered me 20-7. Hey, at least I scored a few points. That was a major improvement from where I was Tuesday!

After D hit an easy three pointer over my outstretched arms, he smiled and shook his head. "You saw that, 'Liyah. I want you to remember this moment because this is a preview of what's to come later on today. Only it's gonna be worse."

"I don't know about all that. What if we win?"

"Well, you'll have me to thank because I worked with you on your game. Plus it's expected that you're good in basketball since you're the li'l' sister of the *great* Damon Anderson! Basketball greatness should come naturally to you."

I smacked my lips and smiled as I picked up my Jordan training bag. "That's exactly like you, D. You're just gonna take my shine?"

He laughed and put his arm around my shoulder as we walked out the doors of the gym. "Come on, 'Liyah! You already know I wouldn't do you like that. But if you even got close to beating us, I'd be proud."

"Aww. That was sweet even though you were throwing shade! I feel you though!"

He laughed. "So what's going on with the rest of the day? Did Alana and Zayy call back?"

"Yes, and I even got them ready to do an interview on your morning show. Then, Dr. Wittamore told us yesterday that the 8th graders were gonna come early for a pep rally, presentation and a quick tour of the school. He obviously wants to make a few of the students who are planning to go to Booker T change their minds."

"That's understandable. He's always forward thinking. But what's going on at Clarkson, Mrs. President? I heard that you ran into a few problems earlier this week."

"A few problems is a major understatement! There were six fights and fourteen people suspended this week. And that was just on Tuesday!"

D's jaw dropped. "You're not serious! *Fourteen* students got suspended? Back last year, that was the size of a homeroom. You kids are bad now!"

"Hey, don't put that on all of us! I'm so much of an *outstanding* student that I got these old, ugly teachers hating on me. They're the reasons why all that drama popped off on Tuesday. How about they decided not to break up the fights or even report them because they were against my new behavior plan that I pitched to the administrators?"

D just shook his head. "That's just how things are with those older teachers down at Clarkson. But hey, at least most of them can actually get up and teach a class right. Howard-Jones has so many clueless teachers! And then these teachers are the ones that are teaching the most difficult and complex subjects like Biology and Math."

I laughed. "Wow, that's a straight up shame! But Miss Carter put all the older teachers in their place. She told them about themselves and then wrote them up."

D was surprised. "Are you serious? Miss Carter wrote them up?"

I nodded. "Yeah, is there a problem with that?"

"If I was you, 'Liyah, I'd watch my back. If you thought the older teachers were checking for you before, best believe there gonna try and get you in trouble now. If it was up to them, you'd be impeached. You're messing with their jobs now. If they get reported again, they could risk getting suspended without pay. Depending on their record, they could possibly get fired and lose their teaching certification on top of that. I'm just giving you a brotherly heads up. Don't get caught slipping!"

D gave me something to think about going into the rest of this year. I didn't realize things would get this deep between me and the older teachers. But hey, it's their fault that they're in this mess. All they had to do was leave me alone and do their job. I know it sounds heartless but it's not my fault.

Like I said before, karma doesn't play!

♠♠♠♠

Familiar Faces

Having Allison along with me for the Howard-Jones tour made things so much better! We picked up on our friendship as if she never was gone. To be honest, I just went along for the Howard-Jones trip and tour because it was something to do. It's a no brainer that I'm going to be a Falcon next year! There was no need to convince me. But, Dr. Wittamore set things up real nice.

When we got off the bus, you would've thought we were about to tour Willowsfield University or some college! I thought the college style feel of the Howard-Jones/Jefferson game was just a coincidence. The first place we went to was the HJ Falcon's stadium where the award-winning Howard-Jones band was performing a few popular rap songs like *Swimming Pools* by Kendrick Lamar and *Mercy* by Kanye West and the G.O.O.D Music crew. They were killing it too!

Dr. Wittamore then spoke to us for two minutes about how great of a school Howard-Jones is and how he wanted all of us who are serious about our futures to become a Falcon next school year. Our teachers then split us up into groups. I was with Dasia, Allison and Jakiyah and Miss Jones was the teacher that was watching over the group. I was cool with that! Ironically, D and Polo were the tour guides for our group. The whole entire tour, they were teasing me about how our team is gonna lose and how Clarkson is, in their words, "too small to even compete". I guess they haven't seen the guys in our 8th grade class. At first glance you'd think they were teachers!

Of course, I had to bump into two of my trifling ex-boyfriends today! When we toured the basketball courts, my "father" and his partner Coach Turner were having P.E. class. My "father" was playing around acting like we got a cool relationship and everything. He was really angering me! Why can't he act all buddy-buddy with me when we're not in front of people? Why did he have to go and cheat on my Momma like that? I played along but I made it to where my time around him was limited. I can only act fake for so long.

Anyway, the students in the class were pretty much just chilling doing whatever they wanted to do. The girls were sitting down talking and texting while the guys were either trying to talk to the girls or playing basketball.

Jakiyah spotted Brandon Roberson right off. He was one of the folks out on the court.

"Aye 'Liyah, look at who that is right there!" 'Kiyah said with a huge smile on her face.

I looked around and saw Brandon. I was confused at first because he was here at Howard-Jones. Last time I checked, he was set to be the captain of Hillman's region championship contending 10th grade basketball team. Now he's at Howard-Jones? I started to get less and less enthusiastic about going down there next year when I saw him.

I shrugged my shoulders and said, "Why should I care? He's probably not gonna say anything to me anyway."

'Kiyah smacked her lips. "Girl, who cares if he speaks to you? You need to stop dwelling on the past. You're at the top of your game now. You got you a cool job and a fine dude you're with. We want him to see how fly you are now. As a matter of fact, you really need to show him how on top of your game you are without him and make sure he gets that message loud and clear!"

"I'm straight, 'Kiyah. Please just drop it."

She put her hands up. "Alright, just tryin' to help you out."

All of a sudden, Brandon shot up a three-pointer that clanked off the rim and found its way over to me. He ran over to get the ball. I picked it and gave it over to him, not even attempting to make eye contact.

"'Preciate it….." He then looked up and recognized who I was. "What's happening 'Liyah?"

I nervously smiled, "Everything's good."

He held the basketball on his right leg, smiled back at me as he looked me up and down. "Wow man, it's been a while hasn't it?"

I nodded. "Yup, a lot has changed."

"You didn't lie about that! What you been up to?"

"You know…things."

To be real, I didn't wanna talk to him. No matter what 'Kiyah said, when I saw Brandon my mind flashed back to when one of my homegirls clued me in on how he was at a Hillman afterparty "chilling" with another female while he was still going with me. Meanwhile, I was at home miserable with a lost appetite wondering if he still cared for me. Mind you, the girl he was with was, and still is, one of the most known jump-offs in Willowsfield. Then, shortly after, I found out about the other girls he was talking to on the side. That straight up broke up my heart!

He caught that I wasn't really trying to hold a conversation and immediately started apologizing to me.

"Hey, I can tell you're still mad about how we ended our relationship. I've been dying to apologize to you but I never see you around. I guess I really took you for granted because of your age. To be real, you're more mature than most of these so called high school females walking around here now. I really made a huge mistake."

"What do you mean by you 'took me for granted because of my age'? You're sitting here acting like you're ten years older than me or something. There's only a two year difference between us, if that. You need to be real, that wasn't the reason why you played me to the side. You wanted to have your cake and eat it too. I wasn't with the game you were running so you went searching for a quick hit, expecting me not to find out.

I then smiled. "It's great that you're man enough to admit that you were wrong about me but an apology doesn't make up for all the hurt and doubt I was facing after we broke up. Thanks but no thanks."

He then nodded his head, "Alright, I feel you. Good luck at the basketball game this afternoon."

After he walked away 'Kiyah, who was pretty much standing behind me when I was talking to Brandon, stepped up beside me and said, "See, that's all I wanted you to do. Tell ol' boy what's up. You did better than I expected! You straight up told him about himself! You're my hero girl!"

I laughed it off, "Whatever, Kiyah. You're crazy!"

The Homecoming Game: Clarkson vs. Howard-Jones

Fast forward to about a few minutes before the game officially started. The rest of the Clarkson students who, based on my new behavior plan, were eligible to go got bussed down to Howard-Jones around twelve o'clock. Everybody was going crazy when Zayy Love and Alana came out and performed before the announcer introductions. I guess people thought I was playing! When I say I'm gonna do something, I do it. Straight up! They tore the house down too.

After a school spirit face headed by Miss Carter and Dr. Wittamore (which Howard-Jones won) and the official player announcements, we were ready to tip off.

Howard-Jones's starting line-up was actually pretty good. You had D at point guard with Wayne Ross, Howard-Jones's cocky, Killa-affiliated superstar running back, as shooting guard. Sean Taylor was at small forward with big, swole Rob Ruben at power forward and my ex-boyfriend that was about to get me jumped, Xavier Johnson, at center. I could tell this game was gonna be interesting...

Our starting line-up was pretty solid too! Of course, I was running point guard and Allison was alongside me at shooting guard. Tay was at small forward, Dwayne (with his old self) was at power forward with Kenyon King, a 6'2", Shaquille O'Neal-looking Clarkson student from 8-3, playing center. Yup, I felt pretty good about our chances.

Until the game officially started...

Each team's players had on similar-colored outfits. Howard-Jones had on black and red clothes while Clarkson had on white and sky blue. Dr. Wittamore and Miss Carter decided to give the players a choice on what colors they wanted to wear out of the differing school colors, since there were so many gang-affiliated guys that were involved in the game.

Howard-Jones somehow won the tip-off and D immediately drove past me and hit a spin move on Kenyon for a smooth, easy lay-up. The Howard-Jones crowd was going crazy! D looked back at me and shook his head. This was more than a li'l' pickup game to him.

One thing that D and I share is a competitive spirit. I brought the ball up court and passed it to Tay. I then ran D off of a few screens. Tay passed it back to me when I made it to left side of our basket and I shot up a wide open three-pointer that swished through the net with ease. D looked at me across the court and smiled. I smiled back and shrugged my shoulders, Michael Jordan style.

The option to wear differing colors based on Clarkson and Howard-Jones's school colors didn't prevent any gang drama from popping off. Later on in the second quarter, Dwayne, Tay, and a few more Rydahz from Team Clarkson got into it with Wayne for throwing up the Killas gang sign and dropping the Rydahz sign after he made a jump shot over Tay that gave Howard-Jones a six point lead. The drama on the court spilled into the stands as other Rydah and Killa affiliated students started getting into it on both sides. They literally stopped the game for something so simple. I swear, it's always something! We can't just have a good time without something stupid popping off.

Dr. Wittamore, my "father", and several campus police officers managed to calm things down before it turned into a full-blown gang riot like back at the Howard-Jones, Worthington High game.

I walked over to D, who was sitting on the edge of the scoring table enjoying the game layoff. D almost single-handedly led Howard-Jones to a 30-24 lead.

"What's good, Mrs. President?" D asked as he rubbed sweat off his forehead.

"I'm angry that they wanna pull all this gang b.s. now. Everything was going cool."

"Come on, 'Liyah! What are you mad for? This is Willowsfield, after all. You should be used to this. Now, what you really should be worry about is how Clarkson is gonna comeback from this seven point deficit."

I smacked my lips and smiled. "We got this, D!"

He laughed. "I believe you! But hey, a li'l' bit of brotherly advice: tell Tay and the Rydah boys to stop ball hogging and play as a team. They're really killing you missing all those stupid jumpers and crazy layups. If anything, you should have the ball. I mean, you are the point guard. You're leading the team in points. Boss up and tell Team Clarkson what's up!"

Even though D was giving me some pretty good advice, I wondered why he was doing it. I mean, we were going up against each other, after all! "Why are you helping me out so much?"

D smiled. "Because you're my li'l' sister and I want you to succeed, even against me. Besides, I want some competition. Clarkson's trying to do too much."

After my talk with D, I led Clarkson on a major scoring run that had us leading 62-58 at the end of the 3rd quarter. For a second, everybody in the gym believed that we could actually pull off a win against D and the Falcon's.

But that buzz quickly died down…

The 4th quarter was crazy! The score was going back and forth. Every time we got the lead, D would take it right back. Team Clarkson definitely wasn't backing down though! We finally were playing as a team. Tay and Kenyon finally decided to step up on the offensive side. Allison was playing lockdown defense on Wayne while Tay guarded D. I switched off him and onto because he was straight up taking me to school! Earlier in the game, he even got a four-point play on me. But things were cool. I was playing some pretty good defense on Sean, seeing that he had only scored two points against me.

It was one minute left in the game and my "father" called a timeout. Clarkson was leading 77-75.

I don't know what they talked about in that huddle, but Howard-Jones came out fired up. As a matter of fact, Polo hit a three-pointer right out of the timeout that got them the lead. A few seconds later, Allison got fouled and hit two clutch free throws that gave us the lead back.

The score was 79-78 with twenty seconds to go. Howard-Jones had the ball.

D ran the clock down to about seven seconds and faked Tay out to get an easy mid-range shot. Howard-Jones once again stole the lead with seven seconds to go and the crowd was going crazy.

We called a time out and made up a play where I would take the last shot. I was honestly nervous! The only thought going through my mind was, *What if I miss it?* Nevertheless, I shook off my fear and stepped up.

Kenyon passed the ball in to Allison from the sidelines. Allison then passed the ball to Tay, who drove into the lane to fake like he was about to shoot a layup. They went for it and he immediately threw me a nice no-look pass. I was wide open at the top of the key.

Two seconds left!

I quickly shot up a three pointer as D approached me to try and block it. As I watched the ball glide towards the goal, I just knew I missed the shot. I just knew it! I felt I didn't aim the ball enough because I was afraid D would block it. I swear, I was ready to beat myself up for blowing the game...

But it turns out that I actually made the shot! We won the game!

I know I was obsessing over a meaningless homecoming basketball game but I have a good reason for why. Afterwards, everybody was coming up telling me about how great I was and how I needed to play basketball for Clarkson this winter.

For once, I finally escaped from D's shadow. For once I was Aaliyah Anderson instead of "D's li'l' sister" and it felt great!

As I look at this custom made MVP trophy that Dr. Wittamore and Miss Carter presented to me after the game, I thought about how fun it was to play the sport that I've always loved and win big for it. Today is obvious proof that I have a li'l' bit of talent going for me! I'm not trying to be cocky or anything; I'm just being real. I may even join Clarkson's basketball team this year...

Anyway, the week started off stressful but ended up exciting and eventful. It seems like things are finally starting to look back up for me after the Allison situation. Life is good right now. I just pray to God that things stay the same over the next couple of weeks when I take the HSAE's (High School Admission Exams). Just looking at the study guide they gave us earlier this week, I probably need to send a few prayers up, for real!

Sincerely,

Aaliyah Anderson

♥♥♥♥♥♥♥♥♥♥♥♥♥♥♥♥♥♥♥♥♥♥

Standardized Tests

November 25, 2012 8:48 a.m.

After how crazy and hectic this first semester has been, I'm glad it's almost over! This entire Thanksgiving break has been about chilling with my family and friends and sitting down somewhere. I've been everywhere over the past few months and my schedule is gonna get even worse going into the New Year.

Clarkson's female basketball tryouts were last week and I actually made the team! To be honest, I was close to not going but Allison, who also got picked to be on the team, convinced me to. After Miss Carter set Mrs. Connor and the older teachers straight about my behavior plan, which will officially go into effect next semester, they've been arguing at me for about everything imaginable. D was right on point. The Teacher Mafia is out for blood now!

Then, the HSAE's have had me going completely crazy! That was last week too. I went to every after school study session that Clarkson had and I still feel like I didn't do my best in math. Math is like my weakness. If I was Superwoman, math would be my kryptonite. What's crazy is that I can help everybody else that I tutor in math but I can't help myself. It may be because Mrs. Rockwell teaches entirely too fast and gets angry at anybody that tries to ask a question, especially me. If I even try and move in her class she'll yell at me.

That's one thing that really angers me about all these hard, crazy standardized test that we've had to take since 5th grade. When we first started taking them in 3rd grade, everything was cool. It was simple addition and subtraction problems - you know, "1+1=2, 10-3=7" and stuff like that. But as we've move up in our grade levels, and as most teachers began to care less and less about teaching, these tests have gotten difficult. Really, what does "1+-9.29/1+z*100" equal? Did we even learn that in class?

I think the whole entire standardized testing craze is just for money. Many people argue that it's racist against minorities, but in this school system, we all fail no matter what school you go to or what race you are. And they love blaming us as students for not paying attention in class or not trying/studying hard enough.

Well, maybe if we had teachers who actually loved the students and tried their best to give the tools that we need to pass these crazy tests we'd do better! Is it my fault that Willowsfield is behind every other city in Georgia when it comes to test scores but above everybody when it comes to sports, fighting, murder, suicide and teen pregnancy? I usually do pretty well on the test they give us. I actually make the city's report card look good. I swear, things definitely need to change in the school system, starting with them firing that stupid superintendent!

Now, I'm not knocking all the teachers. Clarkson has a few teachers that do their jobs very well and get paid next to nothing for it! Miss Jones had us completely prepared for the Reading and English/Language Arts parts of the HSAE's. She's actually the perfect example of what a teacher should be! Miss Jones came to every test study session and stayed until we were sure we'd all get at least a ninety. She was reviewing with all the grade levels too. Now that's a super woman right there!

To prove that I'm not just complaining, when I took the reading part of the test I felt like I got every question right. It's the same thing with the English/Language Arts parts as well. But on the flip side, I felt like I missed almost every question on the science, history, and math exams. I wasn't confident that I'd pass those tests at all.

That should tell you something…

♠♠♠♠

Holiday Events

Like every other year, Thanksgiving was fantastic. Actually, this year was slightly better than all the other Thanksgivings I've been a part of. It started off with the Thanksgiving Parade in Atlanta on November 17th. Usually we don't get a chance to go, but Momma had to do a few promotional stops. Her first book, *Just My Thoughts: The Natasha Anderson Experience* was hitting stores in a few weeks and she was slated to go on a few radio and talk shows in the ATL. She decided to bring D, Faith, and me along. Momma even let us invite Deangelo, Theresa, and Alana.

Speaking of Alana, she's been choosing up on D for a while and I gave him the heads up a few days ago. Honestly, I expected it not to work because of the fact that Alana is a celebrity. D likes to keep things low profile and I thought Alana wouldn't like that. She's not too flashy, but she likes to be seen. Homegirl is a true showstopper!

But I was definitely wrong. Alana is obsessed with D! I guess he laid good game on her that she isn't used to with all the airhead young male celebrities that try to get with her. I'm not sending shots, but it seems like they're overconfident and obsessed with themselves and how much money they have. Then they try to fight, smoke, and wild out like they're from the hood or something like that. That definitely isn't cute!

Anyway, we all had a great time. After the stops at the TV and radio studios and the parade, we went down to Gladys's Knight's Chicken and Waffles. We definitely need one of those in Willowsfield! That food was great!

Then we went to the Thanksgiving carnival down in Willowsfield the next day. Momma was on her way to New York so Ms. Johnson drove Faith, D, and me. This time, we went with a whole crew of people. We went with Allison, Dasia, 'Kiyah, Polo, Deangelo, Wyatt, Victoria, Lyric, Blaze, Keith, Sean, Wayne, and a few more people from Howard-Jones and Jefferson that I can't even name right off.

I don't know why but everybody comes to the carnival with a large group of people! It's always crazy to me. There was a group of teenagers around our age from the Westside that were forty people deep. It always gets me paranoid when I see that. I mean, I know for a fact that fifteen Killas dressed up in all red didn't come down to get on the rides, listen to the untalented pop bands they always have performing, and eat the greasy, unhealthy, high-priced food the carnival sells. No, they came to make a statement and get into some drama!

It didn't help my nerves to see what one of the Killas posted on Twitter earlier that day:

"@Killas4Lyfe @WestSide @OG Butler @GeahLyfe yea we gon' light up the Thanksgiving carnival on Sunday. Like fireworks, G llh #WestWillowsfieldLife"

I guess Willowsfield Law Enforcement got a hold of that Tweet because there were police officers everywhere. Even the SWAT team decided to make an appearance. Most of them were white and had to be racist. The whole time, they were staring us down like they wanted to pop something off! Out of everybody, did we look that suspicious? I swear, racial profiling is real!

Surprisingly, everything went cool at the carnival. Realize that I said *at* the carnival. Boy, I heard things were crazy at the after party though! People started fighting like ten minutes after the Peachtree Street Party officially started. Shots were fired. Fortunately, no one was injured.

But, like D said, that's just how things are in Willowsfield.

♠♠♠♠

Author Dreams

On November 19th, the morning was normal but different at the same time. Like usual, D woke me up at around five o'clock but it wasn't to go and play basketball. Instead, we walked down to Starbucks. Usually, I stay away from Starbucks because their prices are crazy high, but D was buying so I was straight. ☺

We both ordered some hot chocolate and then went to sit in a booth in the back of the shop. D wanted privacy for some reason. We didn't get it at first because everybody that came into the Starbucks was coming up to meet D, congratulate him for winning the region football championship in Memphis last week, and get his autograph. After he signed several autographs and received numbers from two pretty high school girls that looked to be seniors, his full, undivided attention was on me.

"I apologize for all that, 'Liyah. We definitely didn't come down here for me to entertain a crowd."

I smiled. "It's okay, Mr. Championship Winning Superstar. I know how things are. You can't walk out in public without people rushing up to you like you're LeBron or somebody."

"Exactly, and it gets annoying after a while. I mean, I enjoy all the attention and props I get, but I don't let it get to my head. After all, I'm just a normal guy. I haven't really even made it yet."

I was shocked he said that! "Haven't made it? Come on, D, you're just being modest now. Did you just see all those people that came up to see you? Don't get it twisted. You *are* the man."

"Yeah, I'm getting recognized but I'm not *the man* until I start getting paid for what I do. If I'm not getting any money in my pocket for all the hits I take on the field or the elbows and hard fouls I receive on the basketball court, I definitely haven't made it yet."

I took a sip of my hot chocolate and nodded my head. "I see what you're talking about."

He chuckled. "I know you do! You get more money than me anyway. The only cash I see comes from Carswell. That's one thing that I've always loved about you, 'Liyah. You stay finding ways to get paid, Ms. Businesswoman."

I smiled, appreciating D's kind comments. That's why I loved him. He always made me feel special no matter what. ☺

"I don't know about the money thing though, D. You save a lot of what you earn and flip it for good things like books and things of that nature. Me, I get all this money from Carswell and the li'l' businesses I run and spend it on movies, clothes, and this expensive iPhone. If you look at it, it'll break. And don't get me started on AT&T's monthly fee. It'd be cheaper to get one of those prepaid phones from Family Dollar!"

D laughed. "That's straight though. At least you know that's not the way to live. You're business-minded for real."

I took another sip of my hot chocolate. "So what is it that you brought me down here for? I mean, there is a reason, right?"

"What? I can't take my li'l' sister out to get some hot chocolate? We've both been going through a lot over the past few months and we just need to unwind."

I playfully smacked my lips. "You know that's not the real reason why! What is it you need to talk to me about?"

D smiled. "Alright, remember what we talked about back at Carswell a couple of months ago? You know, the whole book thing?" I nodded. He continued on, "Well, I've finally gotten finished doing all the proofreads and revisions to my manuscript and I want you to be the first person to read my final draft."

"Wow, that's great, D! Print it off and give it to me when we get home. I'll finish it by the end of the day."

D nodded. "I can make that happen."

"So what's up with the publishing plan? If I remember correctly, you were thinking about self-publishing."

"I was thinking about that, then I thought about how we're gonna distribute the books, how we're gonna get them in stores, and how we'll know if people will even buy them."

"Come on, D! Didn't we just talk about this? You're Damon Anderson! Your name alone could sell at least about one thousand copies then you have a radio show and segments on nationally syndicated TV and radio shows. You're bound to be a bestseller!"

He thought about it for a second. "That is true. I already secured the copyrights for the manuscript. Do you think I would be able to get it to a big name publisher?"

At first I looked at him like he was crazy. Obviously he forgot who our Momma was. She had just arrived in Miami to promote her book, after all! He must have also forgotten that Roxanne is an accomplished author signed to a major publisher too. We have a bunch of networking connections. After I suggested he try to talk to Momma and Roxanne's publishers, he disagreed.

"That would be a solid idea but we don't know how much influence they have within the company. Besides, when you're dealing with people in the business world, you can't just rely on your last name. You have to bring something more to the table. To be real, the only thing I'm bringing is a city of fans that'll support me in whatever I do. Maybe you can count the fact that I have a two semi-successful radio shows, but that's it. If I was to step to them with no serious writing experience under my belt, they'd probably laugh me out the building."

"Listen, D, don't even stress about all this. Since you finished the story, you can just chill. Let me run the business side. I'll find some way to get you published. I won't even rest until we see your name on a book cover - designed by Karen and me, of course."

D was surprised. "You'd go that hard for me?"

"What kind of question is that? You are my big brother, after all. Just call it payback for all the times you've been there for me and helped out when I was facing tough times. We're gonna make this a team effort!"

Seeing D so passionate about something made me wanna help him in any way I could. Like I said, he's been there for me since day one. Why can't I help him for a change? Mark my words, D's book will be published by next year. I don't know how, but trust me, *Street Love* will be on store bookshelves in 2013! Look out for it!

♠♠♠♠

Elijah Anderson

After we got back home, I immediately went to the den and prepared to watch the re-run marathon of all my favorite black shows from back in the day. I'm a true nineties girl! Carswell bought the syndication rights to air shows like *The Proud Family*, *One on One* and *Moesha* on their TV stations. I was ecstatic when I heard about it too. I'll take my shows from back when I was younger over the junk that's on TV now any day!

At around eleven o'clock, I got a call from Elijah. Like any time Elijah tries to get in contact with me, I was surprised. I answered the phone on the second ring.

"Hello?"

"What's up, 'Liyah?"

I smiled. "Hey, stranger. What's going on with you?"

"Nothing, I'm just cooped up in Pop's house trying my best to stay out of trouble. Jeff went out with his people earlier this morning to maybe hit a lick and put in some work for the set."

I shook my head. Jeff's going to learn one day that all the stuff he's doing is stupid. It seems like Elijah's wising up, though, and that's cool with me. ☺

He then asked me. "Aye, 'Liyah, do you think you could drop by the crib today? You know, we could have that brother/sister day that you were talking about the last time we saw each other."

"Um…yeah. Is our 'father' home?"

I heard Elijah laugh. "Come on, 'Liyah. Think about it. Is that man ever home?"

I grinned. "You got a good point. I'll be down there in an hour. Maybe we can go out somewhere. Is that cool?"

"I'm down as long as you're paying. Staying out of trouble doesn't really get you money like that, you know what I mean? My pockets are flat right now."

I laughed. "Don't worry, li'l' brother. I'll take care of that."

After we hung up, I got in contact with the car service that Momma got for Faith and me the day that I told her that we were related. I ordered the nicest limo that I could afford with the money that I had. I wanted to make our day out as special as it was with Faith.

And it was!

When we made it to Hillyard it was about 11:47 and Elijah was sitting on the porch in a rocking chair. As I looked out the window at him, I realized how handsome my li'l' brother is. Well, I didn't *just* realize it, but I made note of it. Even though Elijah was in 6th grade, he was taller than me at 5'6". It looks like he gained a couple of pounds of muscle since I last saw him too.

His outfit was clean too. Elijah had on a blue and white Adidas track suit with the matching white and blue Samoas. He was sporting a white G-Shock watch with a gold chain around his neck and diamond stud earrings in both ears. And he had that old school Gumby fade that 2pac had in the movie *Juice*, a haircut that just came back in style. I don't know how though! But Elijah looked nice with it.

We pulled up in the driveway and I hopped out the front.

"What's up, li'l' brother?" I said after he got up and walked up towards the all-black 2011 Lincoln Limousine with his jaw dropped to the floor.

"Dang, 'Liyah! We're riding like this today?" I nodded with a smile. He inspected the limo. "Wow, man. This thing is beautiful! Moms rented this for us?"

"For your information, I paid for this all by myself. You don't have to be a rapper, actor, or entertainer to get money."

"That's what it seems like nowadays. The hustlers, dealers, and sellouts are the only ones that ride fly like this."

I decided not to respond to his comment. I didn't want him to feel like I was lecturing him.

As we rode to the northside to go to Chili's, Elijah and I talked about everything. We were having a great time too. It was nice hanging out with my li'l' brother. I wish I would've realized that sooner. Maybe our relationship would've been better. But that's neither here nor there.

The whole time we were in Chili's, I caught several girls looking our way and checking him out. Elijah even caught on to it.

"Hey, 'Liyah, do you see those females over there looking at me?"

He motioned his head over to a group of four girls sitting in a booth. I glanced on the right side of me and nodded as I chewed up a fry. They were cute, but *way* too old for him. They looked like high school girls. He grinned and said, "Do you think I'd be able to hop down on 'em? I mean, they acting like they're interested and everything."

I smacked my lips and smiled. "Boy, you need to sit your young self down somewhere! We didn't come in here for all that."

He laughed and held up his hand. "Hey, they don't know how old I am!"

I know Elijah's a boy and it's seen as a come-up to talk to an older girl, but I had to shut that down! You can't do that in Willowsfield, especially with how crazy these girls are now days! I don't care how old Elijah looks. He wouldn't be able to handle the drama that these high school females bring to the table at his young age. Trust me, I know! I guess you can call it "sisterly instinct." ☺

After we were done eating and we got back in the limo, Elijah smiled at me and said, "Thanks for taking me out like this, 'Liyah. It really means a lot to me."

"Don't mention it. I apologize that it took so long for us to do this."

"Naw, it's cool. I'm loving every minute of it." I then said, "I also apologize for us not having that much of a great relationship with each other. I totally place blame on myself. But, just know I want us to change this. If you ever need to talk about anything, I'm always here."

"I appreciate it, 'Liyah. I've needed someone to talk to for the longest time. Things have been rough out here, man."

"Why do you say that?"

"Sometimes, I just don't feel like I belong. That's why I'm always out in the streets wildin' like I do. I'm just tryin' to fit in. Even in the family, I'm like the forgotten child. You, D, and Jeff are known all around the city. I just get it however I can get it. You know what I mean? I know some of the stuff that I do is wrong. I know I hang with the wrong crowd. But what else can I do? The Rydahz just made it feel like I belong. It felt like I am a part of a true family." He looked at me. "I'm glad I finally have someone to talk about this with. Yeah, I hang with Jeff 24/7, but you know that he's not the type of guy that you talk to. D was cool to talk to, but I don't see him anymore. Dad's never around and Moms is doing her own thing.

"To be honest, I felt like you didn't really like me like that. That's why I never talked to you. I'd just let you guys do your own thing while I go out and find the answers to the questions I have myself. 'What was I put on the earth for?' 'What am I supposed to do with myself outside of do this thing in the streets?' I didn't find out my answers. But one thing's for sure: I know that I'm done with all this street b.s. I can tell already that it's not gonna get me anywhere. But, what do I do to start over? And don't give me that 'give your life to Christ' talk either. I want some real solutions that'll work for me now."

I tried my best to hold back tears. He really laid it all out for me and now he was asking for my help. I processed what he said for a few seconds then said, "The first thing you need to do is stop thinking negative. You are here for a reason. I felt the exact same way you feel, Elijah. I felt as if I was only standing in a huge shadow that D and Momma were casting over me. But with the things I been through over the past few months, I've grown mentally. Even the election changed the way I look at things. We have to find out what you like to do and turn it into an alternative to doing destructive things like being out in the streets. I hate to say this, but Jeff isn't really the type of person you really need to be hanging around. When you're trying to change, you have to cut some people off from your circle. Trust me, I've been there!" I let out a sigh. "Also, I want you to know that I love you. As of right now, we're burying this whole brother/sister rivalry thing once and for all. We need each other, no matter what. I don't care about what our "father" and Jeff do. We need to stay together."

He smiled and said, "I hear you. I love you too, big sis."

I moved over to his side of the limo and gave him a huge hug and a kiss on the cheek. All this time, I thought he was the only one that needed to change. I remember when I was watching *T.I & Tiny* and I wished he was more like Doomani. However, I now realize that we both need to change for this new brother/sister relationship to work. I just need him to be the best Elijah that he can be - not Doomani, not 'Li'l Blue', just my li'l' brother Elijah. Meanwhile, I'll work to try and be the best big sister that I can to him.

I thought it was only appropriate, after we shared this great moment and everything, for him to go and meet Faith. We were on the way back to east Willowsfield. I asked the driver to turn around and go back to Brentwood.

Twenty minutes later, we were in front of Ms. Johnson's house. The first thing that Faith did when she met Elijah was give him a huge hug. Seeing that beautiful sight, I couldn't hold back my tears. I literally cried tears of joy

When she said, "It's so nice to meet you, li'l' brother," it was over for me!

This Thanksgiving was all about family. I was trying my best to reconnect my family the best that I can. I had the driver take us all back to Momma's house. I got a chance to see the rest of the old school black show marathon while Faith and Elijah sat in the kitchen and made up for lost time. And they sat there and talked until it was time for Faith to go home!

♠♠♠♠

Thanksgiving Day & Black Friday

Thanksgiving Day was pretty much normal. All of our aunts, uncles, cousins, and other relatives decided to come down to Momma's house and have a big family reunion. Well…it was more of a "get together and eat all of our food" kind of event. We didn't have anything left over! I was extremely angry because Momma's red velvet cake is the bomb! I guess our greedy cousins thought the same way, as not a crumb was left. She made two huge pans of it too! When everybody decides to come over for Christmas, we have to make sure that they know to bring their own food.

In other news, Faith fit in perfectly with everybody. She didn't wanna come at first because she was afraid our relatives would shun her. The opposite happened though. It took less than five minutes for Faith to be integrated into the already huge Anderson-Smith family.

After Thanksgiving, Black Friday came around. After all the work I've been doing, I was ready to shop until I dropped, for real! I was with Dasia and 'Kiyah going to every clothing store around Willowsfield, trying to catch a good deal. Maybe next year I'll just order my stuff offline…

One thing about Black Fridays in Willowsfield is that they're always ratchet. Momma drove D, Faith, and I down to the Willowsfield Mall on the westside after all of our relatives left the house. Every Thanksgiving after the official family dinner we go down to stores like Best Buy to see how long the lines are.

At Best Buy, people had been camping out since Tuesday. It wasn't that shocking or surprising to me because they do that every year. But then we drove down to the Footlocker outside entrance at the Willowsfield Mall and were instantly stunned.

Nike was re-releasing the same Jordans that had people going crazy back in September, only it had different colors. I kid you not; the line was so long that they surrounded the mall. The people in the far back even brought a grill along with them! They were heating up burgers and steak when we passed by them. They even had the nerve to look at us like we were crazy as we slowly drove past!

And don't get me started on when the stores actually opened. Black Friday clearly showed everyone that Willowsfield is ranked the number one most dangerous city in America for a reason! Some rednecks shot up a restaurant because they received bad customer service close to the Northside Mall Complex. We were down there when it happened. The police shut the whole block down!

A riot popped off at the same Footlocker that we drove by the night before. Like always, they ran out of the new Jordans and the many people who waited for hours to get their pair left empty-handed and angry. A riot literally happens every time they release some new J's, but this one was exceptionally worse! The customers started destroying the store and fighting each other. Somebody started firing off shots and everybody down there went crazy. We drove by that Footlocker again after the day was over and it looked like a hurricane ran through it.

I just shook my head. As black people, we definitely need to do better!

Even though all that happened on Friday, I still made out with some cute clothes and shoes. For the first time ever, I had a good amount of money left over to save! I know D would be proud of me for saying that. ☺

It's safe to say that this break made me ready to take on the rest of the first semester. After all the fun I had, I know for a fact I'm ready to power past anything Mrs. Connor and the rest of the people that hate on me put in my way. I'm also ready to further repair my relationship with Elijah. Anyways, let me go on and go to sleep. The Clarkson girls' basketball team's first official practice is tomorrow and I need rest up so I can wake up with D and work out with him.

Randall Barnes

Sincerely,

Aaliyah Anderson

♥♥♥♥♥♥♥♥♥♥♥♥♥♥♥♥♥♥♥♥♥♥♥♥

New Year's Resolutions & the

Lunchroom Riot

January 1, 2013, 11:24 a.m.

Happy New Year! Wow! I can't believe it's 2013 already. Time goes by so fast. It feels like just yesterday I started 6th grade and now I'm a few months from high school!

One thing that I'm definitely gonna do this year is keep my New Year's Resolutions. For some reason, I always have a problem doing that! Every year, I strive to be more calm and not allow things to get to me so much but I usually forget that resolution my first week back in school from the Christmas break. This year, I'm going make sure that I keep that promise to myself! I'm not gonna let Latasha or any of those teachers get me down. Not this year! I'm going to enjoy my last semester in middle school!

Another one of my New Year's Resolutions is to get D's book pub-lished. I haven't forgotten about that! I started making moves to-wards that goal by allowing my Auntie 'Nessa and Miss Jones to edit it. I was gonna contact a professional editor, but I thought about our budget. Why pay $800 dollars for something I could get done for free? Auntie 'Nessa worked on the grammatical side of the story while I had Miss Jones read it to see if the story itself was good. It's safe to say that Miss Jones was impressed!

"Wow! Damon really wrote this?" she called me up to her desk and asked during 4th period of the last day before Christmas Break.

I nodded and smiled. "Yup, he wrote all of that. D put hard work into finishing it too."

"I can tell! That's one of the most unique and well-written stories that I've ever read. He really needs to get this published. *Street Love* could be a best-selling classic if it gets marketed right!"

"That's the problem. We haven't found any luck with getting any-body to publish it. D's sent queries to a lot of publishing houses. I even convinced him to send it to the publisher that our mom is un-der, and they've turned him down. I wanna live up to the promise I made to him but I'm afraid that I won't. Come to think about it, we're really too young. Book writing and publishing is a grown person game anyway."

"Don't talk negative like that, 'Liyah. A story this well-written is bound to get picked up and published. Just keep pushing on. If all else fails, try out self-publishing. If you need any help, and I mean anything, just come find me."

I smiled. "Thanks for the support Miss Jones. It really means a lot."

See, that's why Miss Jones is my favorite teacher! If anything, her encouraging words made me even more ready to find someone to publish D's work. If we had more teachers like her, the school system would be a better place.

Speaking of school, the last week before Christmas break was crazy. My behavior plan actually has been working pretty well. The number of write-ups is starting to steadily decrease, just as I expected. The overall grades of students have improved too. The Teacher Mafia has been silent ever since the true statistics have come out.

However, the 7th and 8th graders decided to wild out for those last few days. There was a 7th grade vs. 8th grade riot on the last day - a full-blown fight in the lunchroom! Because of all of my responsibilities now, I've been pretty much out of the loop of what's been going on in Clarkson. But 'Kiyah and Theresa caught me up on what happened.

Every year there's a discussion that goes around the school about who would win in a fight: the 7th graders or the 8th graders. Usually, there's a li'l' bit of tension between the guys of the two grade levels, but nothing happens and it dies down after a while.

But not this year! Statuses were posted on Facebook and Tweets were posted on Twitter about the whole entire situation. That made things slightly worse. Then, that day in the lunch room, words were exchanged between some 7th grade Killas and some 8th grade Rydahz. They started fighting each other and then pretty much all the other guys from 7th and 8th grade just jumped in and started a riot.

It's funny because Mrs. Connor and the Teacher Mafia tried to find some way to pin it on me but I wasn't even in the lunchroom when things popped off. Faith and I were in the front office helping Miss Carter and the office staff in getting the report cards organized by grade level and class. I couldn't have stopped them if I tried anyway. How am I gonna prevent a school wide riot from happening? The school president thing only goes so far. I am a student, after all!

In the end, the Willowsfield police department was called and arrests were made. Miss Carter was heated at the teachers. She believed that they could've possibly prevented this from happening. Considering what went down in November, they probably could've. However, Miss Carter couldn't get too mad as they did get in contact with the campus police immediately after things started getting crazy.

To be honest, I'm worried about Miss Carter. I know that that entire riot was gonna be blamed on her somehow and she'd get in trouble. But one thing that I've learned about Miss Carter is that she's a fighter. She'll get over anything that the Willowsfield Board of Education will try and throw at her. If you were to think about it, it wasn't even her fault to begin with.

♠♠♠♠

Christmas Day

Christmas was both fun and hectic at the same time. All morning D and I were hopping around from place to place doing stops at local charities. Then, we went down to Clarks & Wade and hosted a party for them. It was the grand re-opening of the skate center, which had been closed down for repairs after the Willowsfield-Worthington riot a few months back.

Everybody who's anybody in Willowsfield was there, from your sports stars like D, Wayne, Polo, Wyatt, and Blaze to your major drug dealers, hustlers, jump-offs and gangbangers like the Bernard Street boys and the Killas. Alana and her older brother Aaron even made an appearance! Fortunately, things remained cool between everybody and there were no fights or confrontations.

We got home right at 5:30, which is when the huge showdown between the Oklahoma City Thunder and the Miami Heat tipped off. It was fun to watch it with D because he's a huge Hawks fan and hates everything that has to do with the Heat. Meanwhile, the Heat is my favorite team. I even rocked a Miami Heat letterman jacket that I bought off of NBA.com at the Clarks & Wade party. D was saying all types of sly stuff too!

The only thing I said was, "Just wait until this evening. We'll shut you up then!"

And the Heat did just that!

They beat the Thunder 103-97 in a pretty close game. D was talking all types of trash after the game too.

"This is just the regular season. It doesn't mean they're gonna win the finals this year or anything like that!"

I laughed. "Stop hating, D! You know they're better than your Hawks. They probably won't even make it to the second round. LeBron's gonna get ring number two this summer!"

After the game, we went over to Auntie 'Nessa's house for Christmas dinner. One thing about Momma and Auntie is that they both can throw down in the kitchen. Grandma taught them well! Speaking of our grandma, she came down to Auntie Nessa's house too. It was so nice seeing them! At age sixty, Grandma still looks as if she's in her forties! I guess the saying "Black don't crack" is true!

Afterwards, everybody went into the family room while I stayed with Auntie 'Nessa and helped her clean up. She gave me some pretty good news regarding progress in D's publishing journey.

"I've been asking around about book publishing opportunities and I happened to hear about a big writers' conference that's coming down to Willowsfield in a week or so. This could be some really good experience for D. He could even meet a publisher there."

My eyes lit up. "Really? When is it?"

"From what one of my sorority sisters told me, the conference starts on the first Thursday in January and ends that Saturday."

"I've heard about those big writers' conferences. Don't they cost a lot of money to get into?"

She gave me a sly smile. "They do, but you don't even have to worry about that, baby. Both you and D will be at that conference for no cost at all. It really pays off to have powerful, influential people in your sorority."

I ran across the table and gave her a huge hug and kiss on the cheek. "Wow! Thanks for looking out for us, Auntie 'Nessa! You have absolutely no idea how much this means to us!"

She hugged me back. "I know, 'Liyah. I know you and D's dedication to putting a book out there is going to eventually pay off. I'm trying my best to help you guys out the best that I can."

It warmed my heart to tell D the good news later on when we got back to Momma's house. I promised that we'd find somebody to publish his book and I'm going to live up to it. D and I are definitely going to be at that writer's conference on January 3rd!

♠♠♠♠

New Year's Eve

New Year's Eve was once again a hectic day! HoodTalk 98.1 was slated to be broadcasted live from downtown Willowsfield all day during the New Year's Celebration parade. We were competing with all the other radio stations. They were out deep too!

D's show went on at four o'clock yesterday afternoon. It was great to meet and great with all of our fans. Who knew we had so many of them? While the rest of HoodTalk 98.1's shows were broadcasted down at the parade, *The Damon Anderson Show* was live at Willowsfield University. D wanted to do something different from all the other radio stations so he decided to take a page from the syndicated show's playbook. His broadcast was a full out event!

There was a step off between the universities' fraternities and sororities, a talent show, and a basketball tournament. Along with that, there were workshops and seminars on money management, college life, violence prevention and various other subjects. Crystal even did a seminar called "How to survive school in Willowsfield". It was great too! I even learned a few things.

Everything was over at eight o'clock and we went directly over to Watch Night at Mt. Zion. I've been to every New Year's Eve church service that Mt. Zion has held since I was a little girl. Momma always said that the best way to start off a year is with some good preaching. And Dr. Smith always delivers.

His sermon tonight touched me more than the others. In his sermon titled "A Spiritual Resolution", he talked about overcoming hardships and bouncing back from tough times. It was like he knew exactly how I was feeling!

"If 2012 was the year for new beginnings, 2013 is the year for victory!" Dr. Smith said in the midst of his sermon. "2013 will be the year to get a major promotion on your job! 2013 is the year that you will get happily married! 2013 will be the year that you'll get closer in your walk with God! 2013 will be the year you'll finally live out your dreams!

"We're going to speak prosperity into this new year! We aren't going to let our enemies and haters get us down in 2013. We're not going to let the obstacles in our way stop us from getting where we need to be, which is to the top of our faith. 2013 will truly be the year for victory! Can I get an amen?"

Looking at my situation in 2012, I totally felt what Dr. Smith was saying. Last year was definitely the year for new beginnings! I mean, I found out I had a sister! But I feel as if I've mentally and spiritually grown so much over the past twelve months. I've had to deal with BS ranging from school drama and seeing Allison in so much pain to finding out about Faith and dealing with my own insecurities. But I've powered through and made it to the new year.

As I listened to the sermon, I looked over at the new people in my life that have made an impact on me: Faith, Theresa, Karen, and Deangelo. Then I looked over at the people who've been with me and have kept me on the right track for the longest time: Momma, D, Polo, Auntie 'Nessa, Jamarcus, Vicky, Lyric, Crystal, Allison, and Dasia. Even Jakiyah decided to make a rare appearance! As I looked at the people I've been blessed to have in my life, I smiled to myself. God's really been good to me. ☺

Deangelo walked out to the parking lot after the service ended. Momma and Auntie 'Nessa were in there socializing with everybody so we stayed out until about one o'clock in the morning!

"Wow, it's been quite a year hasn't it?" he asked me.

I laughed. "You didn't lie about that! But, like Dr. Smith said, we've made it through in one piece."

Deangelo smiled. "You know something I've never understood about New Year's Eves, especially in Willowsfield?" I shrugged my shoulders. He said, "The reasoning behind the people shooting their guns in the air. I mean, it's pretty crazy to me."

I laughed. "I guess that's their own personal New Year's tradition. It may symbolize something. They maybe want to start off their year 'aiming high' or 'shooting for the stars'."

He laughed. "You're a fool, 'Liyah! But aye, what's our personal New Year's tradition gonna be?"

I smiled wide and shrugged my shoulders. "I don't know…what do you want it to be?"

He smiled and licked his lips real sexy. "You know, they say that the person you kiss at twelve o'clock is the person you're gonna be with for the rest of the year. I mean, if you don't want to I'm cool with it, but…"

I smiled at him and just nodded. A few seconds later, when the clock struck twelve, I pulled Deangelo close to me and gave him a passionate kiss as the fireworks went off and the King Street bangers let off their gun rounds. Me and Deangelo's first true kiss: a New Year's moment that I'll never forget ☺

Well, Thursday is the day that writing conference starts I can't wait! We're going to see if we can find somebody that can help us make D's dream of getting published more obtainable. The whole morning, I kept replaying what Dr. Smith said in his sermon in my head.

"If 2012 was the year for new beginnings, 2013 is the year for victory! 2013 will be the year that you'll get closer in your walk with God! 2013 will be the year you'll finally live out your dreams! We aren't going to let our enemies and haters get us down in 2013. We're not going to let the obstacles in our way stop us from getting

where we need to be, which is to the top of our faith. 2013 will truly be the year for victory!"

That's gonna be my motto for this year. Nobody's gonna stand in the way of the goals I've set for myself. Mark my words, I'm gonna succeed by any means necessary. Believe that!

Sincerely,

Aaliyah Anderson

♥♥♥♥♥♥♥♥♥♥♥♥♥♥♥♥♥♥♥♥♥♥♥

Randall Barnes interviews Aaliyah Anderson

My sit-down with Aaliyah Anderson was rather tense and somber this time around. Several occurrences have happened around Willowsfield since the ending of the second book, none more galvanizing than Miss Carter getting indefinitely suspended from her position as Clarkson's principal. I talked to Aaliyah about this situation, among other topics concerning Willowsfield and the occurrences chronicled in her latest diary entries.

RB: Thank you for joining me again for an interview Aaliyah. From what I've heard, a lot has changed since our last conversation. Talk about that for me.

AA: (Sighs) Well, the biggest change is Miss Carter's suspension by the BOE for the fights that went down back in the first week of November and the big fight between the 7th grade Killas and 8th grade Rydahz. Mind you, none of those incidents happened on her watch yet she still has to take the fall for it. I honestly believe it isn't fair. Miss Carter is only one woman. She can't be in ten places at once but, because of her previous success in the music industry, expectations are high for her. There's nothing wrong with folks expecting greatness out of her, but how can she possibly live up to these high standards when half the folks that work under her don't like her and want to see her fail?

We already know about the Teacher Mafia's beef with her but it's been revealed to me that Mrs. Hudson is against her on the low too. I heard about Mrs. Hudson's dislike of Miss Carter from an incredibly reliable source too. When the two administrators of your school can't see eye-to-eye, that's a problem. Honestly, it's a bigger problem than any drama or trouble we as students get into.

RB: What you just said is a great point. It seems as if all the dysfunctions in the school systems of America are piled on the shoulders of the students. Looking at the situation at Clarkson, is that a correct narrative?

AA: Not at all. The last time I checked, it's understood that teachers have more power than the students. Why are these teachers acting so helpless? Is it that hard to keep control over your class and demand respect without belittling your students like Mrs. Connor and the Teacher Mafia do daily? If these teachers are so scary, why did they even choose to be a teacher? I'm starting to believe that their complaints, while sometimes they're warranted, are just excuses for why students aren't successful in learning what's in the curriculum.

Let's just keep it real! A successful school has structure. That means the administrators and teachers are on the same page when it relates to what occurs in the school. Clarkson is so disorganized and it isn't Miss Carter's fault at all. It's not the student's fault either. We're just a product of the chaotic atmosphere of the school. If some girls have the freedom to jump on somebody without the teacher calling the office for backup, you don't think that fight isn't going to go down? Some of these teachers are just petty and childish! We saw that with how Mrs. Connor did me over the behavior plan. She'd let that poor girl get beaten down in an attempt to prove that my behavior system plan, which actually reduced write-ups, isn't effective. Teachers like Mrs. Connor and the Teacher Mafia are the reasons why these school systems are so messed up. That's real talk too!

RB: Ok, let's move on to another subject that folks really want to know about. What's up with you and Jakiyah?

AA: 'Kiyah's still cool with me for now.

RB: Why do you say 'for now'?

AA: (She folds her arms and shakes her head) Like I said in the story, she keeps on disappointing me. It's not that hard to stay out of trouble but 'Kiyah acts like it's impossible. This girl was going around literally stalking those girls that jumped on her just so she can get a rematch with them. I told her that her plan was stupid and she ended up in jail when it was all said and done. Let's not forget that I had to post bail for her too!

To be honest, I like helping people. I feel like I have knowledge, information and game that can really give folks clarity about certain situations but folks don't listen. I get tired of that! I'm nobody's fool and I'll stop trying to give you advice when I see you keep making the same dumb mistakes over and over again. As a matter of fact,

I'll even start avoiding you altogether because I don't want any of that negative energy to come over to me! Time is money to me and I really don't have the time to waste it.

RB: So is it true that, as the story rolled on, you were starting to distance yourself from Jakiyah?

AA: I was but not deliberately. It was more of a subliminal thing. The law of attraction was in effect for real! I just stopped calling her and hanging with her in school. I didn't have beef with her or anything, I just didn't feel like dealing with her mess. Dasia and I started back hanging together heavy just like back in the day, I was trying to build my relationship with Faith and I had to deal with my work at Carswell, the election and my own school and social life so I didn't really get around to seeing her for a long time.

She felt a certain type of way about it but I told her what was up. She was especially bugging over that thing with Dante. She's the main one always trying to give me advice on guys but she was sweating a boy that didn't even want to talk to her anymore because of how crazy she acts. Dante isn't dating Allison because she's white. As a matter of fact, that's what was preventing him from talking to her at first. Remember, he thought she wasn't up on black guys like that. So, to call Dante a "sell out" was insane and is a perfect example of how childish she is. That's why he's stopped liking her. But, I say again, she has everything to say about my situation! She needs to get herself in order!

RB: The thing I find ironic about your relationship with her is that she always finds the time to put her two cents in on what you have going on and, even though you don't like it, she always ends up being right.

AA: (She smiles and shrugs her shoulders) I mean, I never said her observations were wrong. She is right about the stuff she tells me but

I just get sick and tired of her always judging me. According to her, every move I make with guys is wrong. I get tired of that!

I love 'Kiyah and I know she means well but she needs to worry about herself. She needs to calm her temper down and worry about getting a more pleasurable personality. If the only thing you can talk about is other people, that's a problem. No intelligent, self-respecting guy wants a girl that's so dense in the head that she can only fight, crack and gossip about people. 'Kiyah's my girl but I'm getting fed up with her. I can easily love and care for her from afar!

RB: Speaking of Jakiyah, you two managed to see your ex Brandon Roberson at Howard-Jones during that tour. Take us back to that moment. How did it feel to come face-to-face with him again?

AA: All the memories of us, both good and bad, came back. It took everything in me not to run and hide from him because how he broke my heart still hurts me to this day. I had to be strong though. I've grown too much to be afraid of anybody, especially someone like Brandon.

RB: When he came over and tried to talk to you, he started apologizing and talking about how mature you were. How'd it feel to get the best of him in that conversation?

AA: It felt satisfying. I finally got some closure in that situation. I finally got the chance to tell him how I felt about our break-up and it lifted a burden off of my shoulders. I refuse to be discounted, especially by 19 other girls!

RB: Let me ask you this question because it's been burning inside of me due to my personal experiences with females. There's a certain undying attraction for guys that hurt you girls the most and I don't understand it. Could you briefly explain why

and give these girls out here some guidance on getting over a bad relationship because how you handled Brandon was tight!

AA: (Laughs) You're a fool Randall! I feel where you're coming from though. You're a great guy and a lot of these girls have been dealing with deadbeats they knew weren't good for them so they don't know how to deal with you. Sometimes, things that are broken are unfixable and we need to realize that moving forward.

I guess our problem is, with the negative guys we get with, we invest so much time into their potential that we feel like it's a waste if we just let them go. Sometimes we're just insecure. We feel like we aren't good enough for the good guys out in the world and, because of this, we put up with the b.s. deadbeats like Brandon throw our way. Just like how guys feel like certain girls are out of their league, there are guys we think will never be interested in us.

One solution is that the females out here need to realize that having a guy is an option, not a necessity. That's what being independent really is! I'm not judging anybody because I've had my own dating troubles in the past but all this negativity that we speak on ourselves isn't the move. We need to come to terms with the fact that we're beautiful and that beautiful young women only aspire for the best. Once we embrace that, good guys will come.

RB: Your quest to become a standout big sister is slowly, but surely, paying off. Faith adores you and Elijah is starting to confide in you. Give us your reaction to that.

AA: (She smiles) It warms my heart so much to see that I'm making progress in doing my part in repairing the family. It seems like our "father" will forever be a slave to sex and that Jeff is lost forever but I can't stress over what I can't change. One of my life goals is to be at least half of the older sibling that D's been to me. That's why I'm vowing to try my best to teach Faith everything I know. She's gonna become a successful young woman, even if it kills me. She's only a year and a half younger than me but that won't stop me from trying to lead her in the right direction. Even if I'm older than her by a day and I'm only her sister by a drop of blood, I'm gonna still make sure she doesn't make any stupid mistakes or do something she'll regret. I'm a year and a half younger than D and I consider him more of a father figure than my actual father to me. Why can't I have the same impact on Faith?

I say the same thing for Elijah too. Our talk that we had in that limousine really opened my eyes. Joining the Rydahz was like a cry for help. I'm going to be checking out for him and making sure he stays on the right track as well. I'm going to get him around D more too. D will definitely be a better influence on him than Jeff. That's for sure!

RB: So what's going on with you and Deangelo? You guys finally made your relationship official and shared that special moment during New Years Eve.

AA: It's been ok. Things were cool for a second then my life started getting hectic with my new job schedule and other things I'm a part of. That separation is hurting us, mainly him. I'm not trying to tell too much of what happens next but you're going to see in the next book...

RB: You beat Latasha in the election! Miss Carter even announced that you won in a landslide. How does it feel knowing that you finally got the best of her in an organized setting?

AA: (She grins wide) I love it! The fact that I won the election still makes me incredibly happy. She tried her best to attack me during her li'l' campaign. That whole entire situation when she dissed me on the school news really hit me in the heart and made me break down. But, in the end, she got what was coming to her! The best young woman most definitely won!

I must admit, the excitement has faded though. Being the student body president really is a full time job. I've basically been standing alongside Miss Carter, battling these crazy old teachers and Mrs. Hudson. Now, Miss Carter is suspended. Trust me, I'm going to get to the bottom of what happened!

RB: In your opinion, what was the craziest thing that occurred in this short time span you've been writing your diary entries?

AA: The whole beef between Willowsfield and Worthington. They took social media gangbanging to an all-time high. I bet the Willowsfield and Worthington PD were sitting back while drinking coffee and eating donuts looking at Facebook, Twitter and YouTube watching all those boys snitch on themselves. Folks don't think now days!

That thing MoMoney did was incredibly stupid too. You're going to talk all hard on the radio but the Green Hill Rydahz, who he swore were fake, pulled up and he instantly folded. A special heads up to all the guys out here: stand by your word. That's the only thing you really have. And stop talking about "female drama". That 300 comment status where y'all were calling out each other and all that was crazy and uncalled for. Like I said, I even doubt we'd carry on like that. We'd hop off Facebook, get a camera and go on and fight each other. These boys that claim gangs and street crews in this city, especially Bernard Street and the Killas, are the biggest attention seekers. They're worse than these disease having jump-offs. (Laughs) God bless all of them!

RB: So what's going on in the next book?

AA: It's the second semester! A couple more months until I'm finally done with Clarkson! There was so much that has happened since the New Year. D is closer and closer to getting published every day. We even managed to get some help from a well-known author. Basketball is actually going pretty well for me too. Speaking of school, the *struggle to pass 8th grade and finally make it to high school has gotten even worse. Like I spoke about before, Mrs. Connor and the Teacher Mafia are currently trying to get Miss Carter fired. They have a chance of pulling it off too. I'm going to break things down in the next book. I promise that they're not going to get away with what they're doing.*

Then, the violence in Willowsfield has reached a major peak. We got somebody getting hurt or shot on a daily now days. Speaking of violence, the police have also caught wind of what went down with Gabriel and are starting to investigate further. And we're going to hear more from both Elijah and Faith. So stay tuned. Things are only going to get more interesting!

Bio

Randall Phillip-Green Barnes is an eighteen-year old author, internet radio personality, public speaker and peer mentor who currently resides in Macon, GA. Randall is already renowned for his positive, realistic, and morally driven writings. His first novel *The Diary of Aaliyah Anderson*, a Young Adult Fiction Book, has garnered over 53,000 reads on Wattpad.com and achieved universal acclaim in other arenas.

Recently, Randall's novel *The Diary of Aaliyah Anderson* was added to the Bibb County School System Libary directory, which allows Bibb County students to checkout the book at their high school. Also it was selected to be on the summer reading list for Raa Fine Arts Magnent Middle School in Tallahasse, Flordia and added to library catalogues in Ohio, California, New Zeland and Canada.

Randall writes for the popular news website *Urban Intellectuals* the relationship blog, *Courting Her* and the literary blog *Straight, No Chaser*. Randall is also the author of the eShort *Riverview High: Circumstances*, which hit number 2 on the Amazon charts in the week of its debut, again coming in right under bestselling author Zane's I'll Be Home for Christmas, which was released the weekend of the debut of her movie *Addicted*.

Randall is the eldest son of Edward Phillip and Dr. Rhonda Barnes. He has one brother, William, and auntie Dr. Luciana Green, who serves as his booking agent, and his cousin Nia. Currently, Randall is a recent graduate of William S. Hutchings College & Career Academy. Along with being a talented writer, Randall also has the gift of public speaking. He won first place in the FBLA Region 5 Public Speaking Competition in January of 2013. Randall also was the first student in the history of his school to represent Hutchings in the Rotary Club Speech Contest.

The best is yet to come for this young man. He's currently a freshman at Fort Valley State University in Fort Valley, Georgia and is majoring in Middle Grade Education, among other extracurricular activities such as being a tutor for the residential writing program.

Randall Barnes

Publisher's Note

This is a work of fiction. Any names historical events, real people, living and dead, or the locales are intended only to give the fiction a setting in historic reality. Other names, characters, places, businesses and incidents are either the product of the author's imagination or are used fictiously, and their resemblance, if any, to real life counterparts is entirely coincidental.

DC Bookdiva Publications
#245 4401-A Connecticut Ave
NW, Washington, DC 20008
www.dcbookdiva.com

www.ingramcontent.com/pod-product-compliance
Lightning Source LLC
Chambersburg PA
CBHW031359250626
47155CB00004B/1335